I0460535

REVELATION

The third book in The Judas Syndrome series

Michael E. Poeltl

Michael E. Poeltl

FIRST EDITION

ISBN 978-0-9813168-4-0

To my family
And all my friends.

Memories are of the ethereal, and not the material world, that is how I know I am forever.

Michael E. Poeltl

Leif Speaks....

I watch an army camp among the trunks of dead trees to the west from my vantage point at the edge of this rocky hill, which was carved from an ancient landscape when the ice fields receded some twelve thousand years ago. The ruined forest offers modest privacy and even less protection should we decide to attack them before they do us. But the Sergeant and I have agreed that we are better suited to defend our position within the walls of our compound, rather than risk openly attacking a group so large and desperate.

My Blank Man is with me now. Blank Man is the name I gave to him when he first appeared to me at the age of six. I can feel his presence. Each time he appears the hairs on the back of my neck and forearms prick up. He is dark, and has no features save what I can make out of his silhouette. His voice is calm and soothing. Mom calls him my Guardian Angel, and he even has a halo of sorts. Not confined to his head, but surrounding his entire being. If I'd given him a face he would have one. But I have not in my twelve years of knowing him.

*****

Some months before I will be faced with the vision of an army at our doors, I find myself staring at the forests within our walls. They contain trees taller than our tallest building: pine, deciduous, fruit bearing, with birds and insects buzzing around. From the dust of my mother's Apocalypse, twenty years later, we have trees planted firmly in the soil. We have reestablished life where it was once devastated by a desperate, deliberate act of violence.

I have led a privileged life in comparison to those outside our fortified walls. To have grown up at all is a gift in the wasteland beyond our oasis. I have learned that life is a gift, and should be cherished, lived and experienced. Though experience often reveals itself as pain in this world, it is still purposeful, it still has its place in the evolution of our spirit.

*****

My name is Leif. I've been told that my father was meant for this end. But my father faltered in his attempt, afraid of this destiny, afraid of himself. It has been made clear to me that I was born to carry the torch - that the spirit of my father lives on in me. Though that phrase may seem cliché, it should be taken literally rather than figuratively. I am the reincarnation of my father. My angel has told me as much. And my mom has confirmed it, pointing out the bizarre birthmark on my right arm. It is a dark line that travels the circumference of the forearm, just below the elbow. Mom says this resembles a wound my father suffered not long before he died.

Part One
Chapter One

I feel that growing up here, on this military base, surrounded by protective walls and people, has helped foster my spiritual growth and make me the man I am today. It has allowed me the time and peace of mind required to meditate. It has given me the opportunity to learn from my long sessions of uninterrupted meditation, so that I can put what knowledge I pull from the spirit world to practice in this world.

For the moment, this tranquil existence must cease, as I have recently turned eighteen, and as a resident of this base, am expected to participate in a weekly military exercise. It consists of venturing beyond the walls of our stronghold, in search of other survivors. This usually takes two to three days, with the soldiers camping out in their vehicles overnight.

What weighs on my mind is that not every away mission is successful. There have been times which can only be described as disastrous: where they've returned with casualties, having exchanged fire with an unseen enemy, or worse, when we've lost the whole team.

I am to sit in on a 'ride along' with a battle-hardened group, some of whom are original members of the team assigned to this base twenty years ago. They have witnessed many horrors over the years: skirmishes beyond our perimeter, the defense of our walls, terrorist attacks that come in violent, random strikes.

I'm not looking forward to this experience, but know it is an obligation. It is a practice that has gone on since the bombs fell, and viewed as a necessary duty to bring in new blood.

My mom has gone as far as asking me whether she should talk to the Sergeant and have me removed from this rite of passage. I have told her no. Some of the residents see me as something of an outsider as it is, though I've been here longer than most. I do not want to give them anymore reasons to see me as different.

Anxiety over the possibility of a gun fight between my away team and an unknown enemy fills my chest. I breathe slowly and shake the adrenaline from my arms.

I have been trained in combat techniques: firing a gun, disarming an attacker, blocking a punch. These survival skills are taught to children ages thirteen through sixteen. Whether I am able to recall these learned skills when the time comes I can't say.

I arrive at the gates of the base and meet the men and women that will fill out our platoon. KC is to be our team leader. His small features and wire framed glasses paired with receding hair line and dark stubble create the appearance of being all at once menacing, yet approachable.

Four others complete our group. I am the only one experiencing this for the first time. Though I know virtually everyone's name on the base, they each extend a hand to me and introduce themselves.

"Gibson." A pale-skinned woman with dark short-cropped hair introduces herself first. I know her by her first name: Jillian.

"Hawkeye," a large, looming man tells me, grabbing my hand. I suppose this is a military nickname, as I know him as John.

Another man, one of the original military personnel, approaches me next. "Palisade," he tells me, "but you can call me Erick."

"I will. Thanks."

"Jasper," says a small thin man, reaching up to take my hand. "I'll be driving."

"Good to know," I reply, having a hard time placing this man.

"Now that you've met everyone, Leif, let's get you suited up." KC directs me to a building nestled under the east tower and takes me inside. Here I see stockpiles of ammunition and body armor. KC sits me down as he picks out a helmet, vest, fatigues and boots for me. I pull them on as they are offered.

"This will be your firearm, Leif." The gun is larger than I would have liked, but I know he would have reviewed my training records.

"A shotgun," I state, taking the heavy weapon from him.

"It gives you the best chance at hitting your target, should it come to that."

"Understood." The thought of firing at something other than an inanimate object gives me pause.

KC slaps my shoulder. "Don't worry, I haven't run into anyone or anything in my last three outings. I don't suppose we will this time either, but we need to be prepared for the worst." He winks at me.

"Thanks," I say timidly as he walks me out to the waiting Hummer.

*****

A few hours into our tour of duty we stop for lunch. We have travelled east today, following a monthly routine. The course we've taken is one of six surveyed eastern routes used since the inception of the away missions. Each plotted course has designated 'safe' spots where food, water and ammunition are stashed.

We exit the Hummer one by one, securing the parameter, careful not to make a noise. This safe spot is located at the center of a devastated village.

KC issues orders. "Hawkeye, take the rooftop. Gibson, you're on the left, Erick, to my right. Leif, you stay with Jasper and protect the truck."

I look at Jasper, who is rounding the Hummer. He grabs my arm and pushes me around to the back.

"Take up this position. Get on your stomach and slide yourself under the vehicle." I obey, thankful for the direction.

I wait, and watch. My heart is pounding against the pavement, my neck craning to offer me a better view of my surroundings. I study the buildings. I had ventured beyond our walls before, but never so far. Being in the middle of another settlement was strangely exciting. Reading about the past and seeing pictures don't allow for the 'feelings' I'm experiencing. Trying not to get too caught up in the anxious energy, I refocus on the mission at hand.

Not long after, KC returns to the Hummer, ushering Jasper and I out of our hiding places. "I've gotten confirmation from Hawkeye that the area is clear. We can eat if you're ready."

Jasper nods enthusiastically. I'm not sure I can eat right now as the excitement of the moment has replaced hunger with anxiety, but I will do my best not to seem rattled.

"Did you know, Leif, this is where the Captain is from, originally," offers KC.

Our Captain was a woman of great presence, but rarely seen outside of her home on the base.

"New Caesar, it was called. See the town hall beside us?" KC points to the dilapidated building to his left. "She was the mayor's daughter - comes from a long line of diplomats."

"That's why the base is still operational," says Hawkeye. "The Captain retained military efficiency, but gave civilians a sense of equality."

I like hearing about our Captain's past and enjoy listening to the soldiers speak so highly of her, and her accomplishments.

"The Captain thinks very highly of your mother, did you know that?"

I am a little stunned to get this information, but not for the information itself. "Okay."

"Strong women both," says Jillian, putting back the last of her water.

"And beautiful," adds Jasper. Jillian sends him a look.

I nod, embarrassed, if not a little confused over their affection towards my mom.

KC interrupts. "We all know the story of your mother's journey, and yours."

"No more heroic than any other survivors I'm sure."

"I wouldn't say that," KC disputes. "Your mother's story captured the hearts of everyone when they heard it, and even years later, when I arrived, it was one of the first I heard."

"Me too," Jillian chimes in.

"It's because it's more than a story of merely surviving, it's a tale of good versus evil!" KC jumps off the hood of the Hummer and swings around to face me. "And you're like this prophet or something, come to save us all."

I feel uncomfortable with his description, and with the others now looking on I feel I must defend my position.

"I'd be happy to see you all at my next meditation class, but don't expect any miracles." The group is silent, until I pull a coin from the back of KC's ear. Everyone laughs, including him.

With the mood now lightened, we pack up. Once we've refilled the rations at the safe spot I hop into the truck. Just as Erick is about to jump in beside me his back straightens and he turns abruptly around.

My heart skips a beat. I sense something is wrong. His aura shows him on full alert. He's heard something.

Erick shouts, "Go, Jasper. Drive!"

Jasper slams his door and fires us up the street. It's just Jasper and me in the Hummer. I turn in my seat to watch as the other four scatter behind a brick fence that lines the sidewalk in front of the town hall.

"We should go back," I say without thinking.

"We have our orders, Leif," Jasper replies dryly.

"Orders? What orders?"

"It may be nothing, Leif. Let them figure it out. We'll pick them up as soon as they've secured the area."

"I thought we did that already. Shouldn't we help them?"

"We have our orders," he repeats.

"What orders?" Frustrated, I go for the door and hear a click. Jasper has locked me in the vehicle. I pull at the handle. "What are you doing?"

"Just sit tight. It may be nothing."

Suddenly an explosion rocks the town hall, blowing what little glass remains out of the windows. I watch as my team huddles against the thin brick barrier, a shower of glass and debris raining down upon them.

"Shit," Jasper spits. He turns the car around.

I'd never seen an explosion like that before and the shockwave passing through my body leaves me stunned.

"Goddamn it!" Jasper is getting jumpy in the driver's seat. I blink and focus on the action beyond our windshield. KC and the others are focused on the town hall but I watch as a body rises out of the street.

Jasper notices too. "Jesus, they're coming out of the manholes!" He rolls down his window, opens his door, steps out and takes aim. Snapping one shot off after another, Jasper puts down the first figure sneaking up on our team. Then Erick turns to face the threat and fires on his attackers.

Soon everyone except me is caught up in the shoot out. I crawl over the bench seats and wiggle my way to the driver's side.

Jasper looks over at me. "Stay put!"

"I can help."

"We have our orders. Stay put." Jasper shoots me a look so hard I forget to ask 'what orders' this time. I lay my gun at my side and watch in horror as figures drop before our team's gunfire.

The fire fight does not last as long as it felt. Within two minutes the attacking sewer dwellers are downed.

Our group frisks the bodies and collects what useful tools they find. KC waves us over. Jasper nods at me and I get out of the truck.

"Don't forget your shotgun," he reminds me.

We approach cautiously. The smell of burning brick and wood permeate the air.

"We need to go down there," KC tells us. "They've obviously made a home underground. There could be more of them, but there could also be valuable items we could use back at the base."

"I'll go," I say if for no other reason than to get a reaction out of them.

"No, Leif," KC tells me.

"Why?"

"We have our orders."

"So I hear. What orders are those, exactly?"

"You are not to come into harm's way."

"A little late for that don't you think?"

"Perhaps, but let us keep you safe while we complete this mission."

"Why bring me out here at all?"

The five look at one another. KC explains. "If we had overlooked you for this you would have lost face with the others. Sergeant Jones insisted we take you out, but made it very clear that you were not to engage an enemy."

"So you're all here just to babysit me?"

Jillian steps forward, rubbing at the spot on her vest where she had been hit. "You're getting your experience, either way. You're out here."

"I guess."

"Let's get this thing done and move on," KC insists.

Hawkeye and Jasper disappear through the manhole. Jillian follows while KC and Erick remain with me.

"Erick, bring the Hummer to us."

Erick nods to KC and rushes past us. Our team leader looks thoughtfully at me.

"Leif, the Sergeant is only trying to protect the base's interests. You are a valuable member of our community."

"We're *all* valuable members," I retort.

"Sure, but there's more to you, and whether you know it or not, we're all counting on that." He lays a hand on my shoulder and ushers me into the Hummer.

I sit in contemplation. I know I'm being groomed by my Blank Man for some greater role. But I hadn't realized others were picking up on it. Perhaps since incorporating the deeper lessons I've learned from my angel into my meditation classes, people have talked.

A moment later Jillian emerges from the hole in the ground. Then, behind her, three small figures appear. She kneels at the manhole, shielding the children from the lifeless bodies of their guardians littering the sidewalk, directing them toward KC and Erick. They seem hesitant, but do as they are told. I step out of the Hummer and approach the children.

"This changes everything," KC says. "We go back to base."

I smile at the children. Their auras illuminate the grey day, though they each wear a grimace. I help them into the Hummer and sit with them. They are nonresponsive to my questions, but I believe they will be all right after a decent meal, dry clothes and a delousing.

After another sweep of the underground, KC is satisfied and Jasper takes us home. Nothing could be more welcome to our community than children.

Chapter Two

I regret the deaths of those children's parents, if in fact they were their parents. I couldn't have made it to where I am without my mom. In fact I am very grateful for all the men and women here. I am grateful for everything we have which those beyond these walls do not. I'm grateful for the new people that find us, either by way of luck or during an away mission. Mom and I were picked up on one of these missions when I was just a baby. *Destiny at work*, she has told me.

Each new survivor is tested and put to work where their talents best suit the base's interests. At the age of sixteen I was tested and given the role of morale officer. It is well suited for my talents and I find the work very rewarding.

I walk the inside perimeter of the base every morning, running my hands along the cool steel plating of the walls that keep marauders out, and those looking for salvation in. The buildings vary within our walls. A massive greenhouse has subsidized fresh fruits and vegetables for the freeze dried and frozen produce that stocks the kitchen's many storerooms and freezers. A stockade, which has housed many a criminal mind, sits adjacent to the front gates, which are heavily reinforced and have a tower guard on either side. The hospital and housing units blend into one another in a stream of dull gray brick. Nothing was built for its esthetic value, but rather for its sustainability and longevity. The material world has not interested me though, save those souls that suffer its harsh realities.

Mine is an old soul. Not only am I the reincarnation of my father, but I have lived many, many lives before this one. To avoid ego, my guide has not revealed those other lives to me, only nodding in response to my question of lives lived.

An old soul carries with it an unconscious knowledge cultured by their past lives. The vast majority of us cannot experience these teachings, but the knowledge is there, and can be drawn on through meditation. Wisdom of the ages refers to the wisdom gained by lives lived. Those that bring the wisdom of the ages to the waking world have learned how to capture that information, and pass it to the masses.

I am told that this knowledge, once gained, will excel the level of mental maturity in the person, causing them to exceed in all areas of study and seem enlightened. My own level of intellectual maturity has both amazed and frightened those around me. I know no different..

My enhanced state of consciousness upsets me at times, as my peers have a difficult time relating to me, and I to them. But I have found my stride, and hold meditation classes for all ages - helping them realize a similar goal of enlightenment. I can't help but wonder though, have I missed out on much of the human experience?

My Blank Man has spoken the names of great religious leaders that taught enlightenment through recorded history, referring to Jesus, Buddha, Confucius, Muhammad, Gandhi, Lao-tzu, Abraham and others. He mentions them, not to build my ego in linking me to them but, rather to build my confidence in their shared vision - *our* shared vision.

So much of what makes up this wisdom still waits to be discovered. The idea of it excites me. My angel has been a great source of knowledge, both that which is locked inside of me, and a wisdom that transcends my own.

Chapter Three

Besides my mom and angel, one other person has nurtured my spiritual curiosity. He is the one man I would like to have called father in my time here. Ironically, that man is a Catholic priest, *Father* Henderson. He is the Chaplain here, assigned this post just days before the bombs. The base itself was expecting a compliment of one thousand soldiers and their families to fill its newly renovated accommodations. But before that could happen, the Apocalypse struck.

In the Chaplain I have found a confidant who speaks at my level of spiritual understanding. Though his is confined to the limits of his Catholic religious tradition, he is a very enlightened individual.

We have enjoyed countless conversations and debates over the years. He has never treated any of my curiosities as trite or made me feel hesitant in asking questions about his own faith. He instead welcomes the arguments and questions, and enjoys feeding my hunger for knowledge. I respect him like no other.

We sit, as we have countless times before, in his greenhouse to discuss a vision, or a piece of information or method of meditation offered to me by Blank Man. The Chaplain doesn't know about my otherworldly mentor: Blank Man's existence is known only to my mom and I. But I suppose the Chaplain suspects someone or something is feeding me spiritually. Perhaps he assumes it is the figure he calls God. Either way he doesn't ask, and I don't volunteer.

"I've said it once, and I'll say it again, Leif. You are a gifted young man." He moves gracefully around a large potted fruit tree with his watering can.

I smile, embarrassed. Sometimes I really want to tell him all about Blank Man, but in sharing the knowledge my angel feeds me, I often do so in the guise of discussions and debate, questions and answers.

The Chaplain is a friend, though forty years my senior. His dark features hide in the shadow of the leafy tree as he rounds it a second time. His voice is deep and yet soft, the perfect mix in a speaker. He holds Sunday service in the mess hall to a large crowd of followers. Not all were Catholic, but they come to be a part of something bigger than themselves.

"You're not looking to steal away the rest of my congregation are you, Leif?" he asks, mock worry wrinkling his forehead.

It's true though. Many are finding my meditations and parables attractive, but this does not distract them from their Sundays with the Chaplain. I have no religion save the betterment of one's self. I offer enlightenment in place of heaven. I teach but never preach. My word has been heard before, but, like so many that have come before me, the words were bent to the will of man. Words thought to come from a God find power in men and power leads to want and want to war and, well, here we are. Nearly twenty full years into an Apocalyptic end. But, will it all *end*? I've only known this life. Aside from reading what paper books are available to me, and in the computer database of our library, I know nothing else.

I watch the Chaplain place the watering can down and manually pump water from one of a dozen wells drilled into the footing of the base.

"I think we should join forces, personally," I kid. He is a staunch Christian and though he appreciates my own brand of spirituality, could never consider leaving his church.

"We've had this conversation." He picks up the can again and moves around me. I turn to watch as he sprinkles the vegetable garden.

"You know, with the increasingly diverse religions I preach to, I think you're becoming more and more accepted by the masses."

"We're not in competition," I remind him. "We both work toward the same end."

"Saving souls," he proclaims, gingerly waving a fly from his tomato plant.

I nod and smile. The Chaplain rests his watering can on a table next to the raised pond filled with tiny fish, and we walk the length of the greenhouse.

"I see myself as something of a renaissance man," he tells me. "Like those great missionaries before me. Going to a strange land and preaching God's word."

Books have explained this process to me and though I respect Father Henderson, I have never found anything admirable in those men: missionaries riding a wave of violence against a "savage" race in a foreign land, destroying their spiritual histories, leveling places of worship and raising crosses in its place.

"You are a better man than those," I reply. "You have embraced other religions."

"Have I?" He stops walking and turns to me.

"You have allowed others to speak their mind," I remind him. "You do not turn them to your faith, but you feed their spirit."

He nods slowly, closing his eyes. "I learned long ago that pushing anyone into anything is counter-productive. If an individual wants to feed their soul I am available. If they want to rationalize God's word I will do my best to talk them through it, and if they want a funeral, I respect whatever faith they decide on and preside over it."

"You see? You're no missionary." My smile ignites his and he slaps me on the back, the sting meant as a reply to my – what he would call - cheekiness.

"If it's all the same to you, I'll do things my way, and you do what you do, because it seems to be working."

Father Henderson resumes his slow, deliberate walk and I follow.

"You know, Leif in all the time we've spent together, in all our conversations, you've never asked me why."

"Why?"

"Yes. Why."

"Alright." I cross my arms and lean against the trunk of an apple tree. The Chaplain watches me with a smile in anticipation of the question. "Why?"

"Why what?" His smile increases ten-fold. I break into a toothy grin.

"Maybe you don't have the answer then. Is that it?" I tease.

"If it has to do with my own faith, Leif, I can answer any question."

"Is that what this is about?" I push away from the tree, my arms unfolding. "Your faith? Why I haven't asked you why you chose the faith you follow?"

"It struck me just now." His hand wipes away beads of sweat forming on his forehead. "You've never questioned why I chose Christianity over other faiths. Why not Islam, why not Judaism, or Taoism or Hinduism."

"It doesn't matter to me. Your faith is all that matters. It has taken you this far, allowed you to preach peace. What difference would it make what you believed, so long as the basis of that faith was compassion and love?"

He sucks in a deep breath. "You are so very wise beyond your years, Leif." His head falls and shakes as he turns and walks toward the fish pond. "It's difficult for me to understand how more than one religion can exist. I mean, I've never been opposed to others' religious practices, but I always assumed I was right – that I was on the right path."

"So long as you follow your heart Father, you will never find yourself on the wrong path. You are a deeply spiritual person, and that alone will take you farther than most. What religion you believe is not what will deliver you into the light, but your actions in this life, and the reactions they set in motion."

"Leif, you make me question my very belief system." His voice becomes hard and distant. His hands grip at the edges of the raised plastic pond, dark skinned knuckles fading to white.

I touch his shoulder. "Father, don't compare one religion to another, or one prophet to another. Prophets are important, always have been. They are the teachers. To understand their words is to follow their light."

"Yes, and I understand my faith, and I understand that virtually all religions vie for the same end, to go to Heaven, or experience Nirvana – it's the same thing. But tell me Leif, why did I *choose* this path?"

"To each their own, Father. Your choice will see you through to that end. To introduce multiple religions is to introduce choice to the people, and all people of the flesh suffer the same end. We will all die, and if we've lived well and done good, as your chosen religion has taught, then whether we come back, or have achieved a level of enlightenment, our afterlife will reflect those actions."

"You talk of the afterlife *and* reincarnation. Which is it for you, Leif?"

"Both. Most will come back, and that too is an afterlife." I knew I was my father before I was me. Had my father followed Blank Man's guidance as I am, I suspect I would not exist as Leif, but rather exist in the spiritual plane.

"But, Leif, I don't want to come back." His back still to me, he hunches over the pond, staring intensely into its muddied waters.

"That will be determined by your actions in this life," I say decisively, leaving no room for discussion.

The Chaplain turns to me and nods slowly, his eyes alight with understanding. His hands float up and away from his sides.

"We're all in this together."

Chapter Four

That evening I sit to meditate in the forest within our great walls and ponder the actions that have brought me to this moment in time. The sun falls behind the west tower, and summer is in full swing. A gentle breeze shakes the canopy of leaves above me. The air is warm and smells sweet as it pushes past my face. I inhale deeply, hold and exhale slowly.

A sharp sting cuts the serenity of the moment as something hard hits the back of my neck. I turn and see three men approach.

"Why don't you do that someplace else?" shouts Harry. He is one of two orphans found beyond Elle Lake just one year before I arrived. He is a hothead and was recently removed from military duty for insubordination. The two beside him are Chris and Monty.

A nervous smile grows on my face, and I wave them over. My heart races as memories of past bullying play on my nerves.

"Screw that," says Chris, wiping his shaved head, which is littered with long thin scars, a result of some horrifying ordeal he'd experienced while on the outside.

"You can take your fairy class and shove it!" Harry spits out.

They are classic bullies, though warned not to disturb me during classes, they are less inhibited when I am alone.

"Throw something back at me, you queer," taunts Monty. He wears a permanent scowl. Something he adopted at age six, after watching his parents be brutally murdered at the hands of rival survivors.

Each has a story. Each has adapted a personality to hide their pain. Fear rises in my chest. I hate that I can't control it.

Harry goes down on one knee and pulls up a chunk of asphalt from the broken road.

"Will you move if I throw this at your head?" Harry squeezes the fist sized piece of debris, and then hurls it at me.

I duck to avoid the flying object but it catches the bridge of my nose and I fall sideways. That's when something snaps inside me. I hear Blank Man in my head, but block out his pleas for a nonviolent outcome.

I grip my nose with both hands and stagger to my feet. Their laughter triggers in me a rage I have buried all these years.

They have come into the woods now, and as I listen to their footfalls on the forest floor I throw myself at one of them. We crash to the earth with a thud and I hear the wind escape the lungs of the man beneath me. I release the grip on my nose and feel a kick to my side, then another, and another. Monty and Chris are pummeling me.

I roll off Harry and kick at the legs in front of me. At the same time I feel a sharp pain to the back of my head as a fist lands a punch at the base of my skull.

Suddenly a roaring voice can be heard over the ringing in my head. The assault stops immediately.

"Step off!" the voice bellows.

"He started it," Monty lies.

Looking up, I see four black army issue boots shuffling the three away from me.

"Are you *shitting* me?" The voice rips into Monty's story. "Leif started a *fight*? Get these three under house arrest. I expected more of you, Harry."

I listen while lying on my stomach in the soft moss, mentally assessing the damage done. My ribcage hurts, but no more than a bruise or two. I pat my nose and pull my fingers away, wincing when I see blood.

I've never been hit before, and hope to never experience it again. A hand wraps around my forearm and pulls me to my feet.

"Jesus, Leif, you alright?" asks the soldier. It's KC.

"I'm okay. I'll be okay, thanks." I stretch and rub at my sides.

"What happened here?"

"I'm as much to blame as they are."

"I doubt that. I'll take you to the hospital and get you looked over."

"I screwed up," I insist, rolling my neck.

"Self defense, I'm sure," he suggests.

KC takes my arm and leads me across the compound and into the hospital.

*****

Why now did I choose to react in violence rather than allow it to pass? They'd never actually hit me before. They'd kicked dirt in my face, pushed me, but it had never escalated to this level of hostility.

Blank Man is as troubled by my reaction as I am.

"That you are distressed by your actions is important," he tells me. "You cannot lead others in peaceful meditation if you yourself exhibit fits of violence."

"I understand. Should I have taken the blow and bowed out?"

"You should have removed yourself from the confrontation the moment it began."

"I see." But I don't, not really. I mean, I'm entitled to sit in the woods just as much as anyone and be left undisturbed. I'm confused. I feel many things, shame, anger, but regret? I'm not sure about that.

*****

With my three oppressor spending a night in the stockade, I return to my corner of the woods to complete what I had started.

Gradually, I steady my mind and visualize Blank Man in front of me. He appears, sympathetic. I let my mind wander and, maybe because of my recent encounter, find myself lamenting my father's struggle.

"Tell me about my father," I say. Mom rarely spoke of him, side-stepping my questions even now. I used to think she was protecting me from some terrible secret when I was younger, but I'm eighteen now, and I want to know.

"Your father, Joel, was one of many chosen to lead in the time after. You are your father, and within you lives the same promise he rejected."

"I understand my father and I are one and the same. But why did he fail?"

"Your father failed because he fought the idea. He could not accept the concept of destiny. He felt he had been robbed of his free will. He attempted to veer from a pre-destined path, and with each determined move, his own destiny became clouded. "

"So he was capable of changing his destiny?"

"A destiny cannot be so easily side-stepped, and your father came to realize that. It is essential in a leader to understand structure and purpose, and that is what I was hoping to instill in Joel, so he could move toward this greater purpose."

"So then what? How did it end for him? How did my father die?"

"I was tasked with bringing him back to the idea of destiny, but failed time and again. I entered his dreams, I appeared to him in the waking world: I pleaded with him to see purpose in the tragedies that had befallen humanity. But he pulled further away from me the more I tried to connect, until the realization that he could never be *the one* was clear. You know of Gareth and the great struggle he brought to your mother's group. Your father had banished him and his followers from his home, the place where you would be born."

"Yes, mom has told me that much."

"Gareth led a group of survivors with a flag that embodied the world before. With this flag and the ideas it symbolized he was able to amass an army that went unchallenged wherever they went."

"Until they came upon my mother's group."

"Yes, Leif. But little did your father know Gareth would play a much larger role in his life. Joel's destiny had irrevocably changed from the path I'd hoped to show him, to the path he had made himself.

"Once we realized Joel could not be *the one* to lead, I planted in Gareth's head the vision of Joel's new path: where your father would come upon Gareth's group once more and offer a sacrifice. This sacrifice would be your father's friend. Driven by a paranoia that had been growing in him many weeks, fed by the narcotics he found himself hopelessly addicted to."

"He had lost his ability to see truth."

"Yes. And so, your mother with child a month prior to the event, we resigned ourselves to the idea of reanimating Joel's spirit in you, his son."

"But how did he die?"

"Once Joel had offered his friend to the will of Gareth, the outcome was clear. Your father would end his own life, and in doing so, allow us to start anew with his son."

This is what the scar on my forearm represented. For the first time, I understand my father had killed himself. The knowledge that my father was a coward stuns and confuses me. I break my position and slouch over. My head shakes from side to side in a slow, deliberate motion.

"I am not proud of the way I handled your father, Leif, but have forgiven myself. What good comes from *this* end is what matters now. What we build from the ashes of your father's choices are all that matters now."

"Does my mom know this?"

"She asked me once if your father was responsible for Connor's death, but before I could answer she withdrew the request to know. It is yours to tell now. If you feel it would serve her."

"I don't see the point, unless it is better to know the truth. Tell me what to do."

"I cannot. It has no bearing on your destiny. This choice is yours alone."

As I meditate on this question Blank Man offers more information.

"Do you remember Earl, Leif?"

Of course I remember Earl. Mom's sworn enemy. Earl had torn her small group of friends apart after my father's passing and forced her to flee their shared home. Then, eight years later, he turned up at our door, here on the base, having put together a rag tag band of desperate survivors. These people would test our defenses and attack our soldiers on scouting missions. Eventually Earl was taken prisoner, and while awaiting execution in the stockade, my angel directed me to talk to him, to 'know my enemy'. I didn't really understand why at the time, but a picture in my head was beginning to take shape.

"Yes, Leif, the events that will come to pass include many more variances than merely guiding you. I gave you that opportunity to meet and speak with your enemy when you were just a child. Now that you are an adult, you will be asked to face this enemy once more."

"Earl is still alive?" The question is more like a statement and I breathe deeply, thinking back to that night in the stockade.

*****

I was eight. The sky was beginning to darken, with stars appearing overhead one by one. Rumblings of thunder coupled with humid gusts of wind blew in from the west, slipping over the high steel walls of our fortress.

I had always enjoyed storms. Though anything longer than a few minutes usually scared me, a quick and powerful downpour was invigorating. I would run into the potholes that lined our streets and kick and jump as they filled with water. Flashes of lightening, rolling thunder and the sting of the driving rain always made me feel alive.

The night I met Earl, however, the rain didn't begin until I was already facing him, my enemy, through heavy steel bars, his hands and feet chained to the wall.

"Know your enemy," Blank Man had whispered in my head. From that moment I felt compelled to walk to the stockade, leaving the daycare, without my teacher's knowledge.

When I arrived, a vision of a key placed behind a loose brick filled my head. Once I had located the brick, I worked the key into the lock and let myself in.

In a dark corner of the stockade, a man sat in a cage. He was hunched over, his breathing ragged. A light in the opposite corner cast heavy shadows on the man and it was difficult to know whether he was looking in my direction or sleeping.

"Who are you?" he asked in a low rumble. I jumped at the sound.

"Your enemy," I answered, my voice pitching higher than I'd have liked.

The man offered a pained laugh at that. "Everyone is my enemy." He sat up and I could hear his chains rattle.

"I know that." I sat on a bench under the light.

"Who are you?" His head tilted to the right as he studied me.

"Leif," I answered.

"You're Joel's boy," he realized. "Sara's kid." He reached for his face but stopped short as the chains pulled taut against the wall. He lowered his face to his hands and rubbed at his eyes.

"You smart like your mother?"

"I don't know."

"She's a smart one, that Sara. You're a lucky kid to have found a place like this to grow up. Listen, we don't have to be *enemies*, you and me," he began. "Your dad and me were friends for a long time. Your mom too. We could be friends like that."

"No, I know that's not right."

"What do you *know*?" He leaned back, rolling his knuckles against his thighs.

"That you are my enemy."

"And where did you get that information? We were *friends*, your dad and me. The best of friends."

"I have a friend who tells me things."

"A friend, eh?" He laughed raggedly. "Listen, Leif, maybe talk to your *friend*, ask him to join us. I'd like to speak to him too."

"No, he won't see you." I stepped closer to the bars. Earl's face became clearer in the light as my eyes focused. He had a terrible scar on one side and a partial beard on the other. His red hair was slick and pasted to his forehead.

"No? Come closer," he urged as a whisper of a smile inched its way up the uninjured side of his face.

I felt myself wanting to obey him. It was a strange feeling. I knew it was dangerous to approach this man, but his eyes drew me.

"You know, your dad and me shared a lot of good times before this end came." He gazed at the ceiling. "We were friends." He looked at me again, still inching closer to the cage. "We did everything together. *We* should be friends."

I didn't doubt my father and Earl were friends at one time, as I could see Earl's aura shift when recounting his pre-Apocalyptic life. I found myself feeling sorry for him. I wondered if maybe we *could* be friends.

A moment later the door to the stockade swung open. A bright light shone in my eyes as two silhouettes pushed into the small space. One grabbed at me as the other shouted something through the bars at Earl.

I remember feeling grateful for having had a conversation with Earl. I felt a connection to my father that transcended the birthmark on my forearm.

*****

I break my meditation and stand. I'm lightheaded and stabilize myself by planting both hands on the trunk of a tree. Its energy feeds mine and I saunter off to my quarters.

Chapter Five

That night I take a detour to my room and walk through the compound. The air is crisp, and as I leave Father Henderson's visionary forest, I inhale the sweet scent of the spongy green moss carpeting the ground.

The night is quiet save the hum of the windmills, as it is most nights, allowing me to reflect. My thoughts tonight find me wanting. So many thoughts vie for attention that it is difficult to pin them all down. Blank Man had explained much to me, but there is more to the story of my father's life that I feel I need to know.

And that Earl is still a threat to our way of life, that he is someone of interest to the other side and that my own Blank Man has hinted at his importance in bringing about my destiny is disconcerting.

Back at my room I have trouble sleeping, tossing and turning as I try to piece together all that I now know of my father. I also find myself questioning my guide's approach to my father's difficulties.

"I've explained this to you, Leif. It is done."

"I'm just - I don't understand why it had to happen that way. Why did Connor have to die?"

"You are here, now, because of what transpired then."

I stare at Blank Man as he materializes beside my bed. Suddenly images of the Reaper, dressed in a heavy, dark cloak, bent over a large console of red and yellow buttons, flash through my head. A world map of hotspots lit up in front of him on a massive screen as his skeletal fingers push at the keys. I recognize the imagery as almost comical in its simplicity, but know the vision is more than just a farce.

"What *aren't* you telling me? There *is* something more."

"You've been struggling with the bigger picture." He'd read the images in my mind. "You're trying to put the pieces together. You feel there is more to the one called the Grimm Reaper; that his role has been somehow understated."

"His ideas – they were aligned with much of what you have taught me. They were noble, spiritually driven and, *enlightened*."

"They were."

"You *knew* this person?" My heart races: the story of the Grimm Reaper is about to be revealed to me.

"We have known of it a *very long* time."

Every hair on my body stands in anticipation. "Tell me."

"You know of what I speak." A pause. "You know what lengths evil will go to in order to perpetrate its own continuance."

"Even an enlightened mind such as his?"

"It's was *not* enlightened, but *enflamed*. It is no man, but spirit."

"Is there such a thing?"

"There is, and they are *many*."

"What spirit would inflict such horrors?" I feel suddenly sick. I feel that despite all I know, all I have been shown, that I've only experienced half of what the spirit world offers. That such an unspeakable evil could exist in a realm of such beauty… I focus again on my angel. The spirit's image twitches as I sense his energy spike.

"It is the great deceiver of man."

"Why wouldn't you tell me this?"

"What information you are offered is a tool for your ministry. Some information you are not meant to have."

"Then why answer my questions?"

"Because you ask them," he says matter-of-factly. "Mankind is such a curious creature. You are so simple, so material, yet so advanced in your processes. You question everything."

"It is one of our strengths."

"It is, and so I do not deny you the answers to your questions, but why question my answers? Why do you not simply accept them and move forward?" I understand his point, but that does not mean I will leave it alone.

"Is this spirit the *Devil*?" I ask.

"It may go by that name. It is *evil*. It is hate, jealousy, malice and guilt. It represents the opposite of everything good and beautiful. The spirit world is not so different from the material world in this respect. There is an opposite for everything, and *in* everything."

"So evil isn't just a facet of man? It's everywhere, in everything?" As the epiphany hits me I sit up straight in bed, clutching the sheets. "It's not the invention of man."

"No, it is not. But it is your choice, and it is your burden."

"Yes, as it has always been." I ball my hands up into fists. Then I release them and force myself to relax.

"Thank you, my friend. Thank you for always telling me the truth - whether I have to ask for it or not." I look up at him and sigh. "I appreciate your friendship and all that you have done for me, and for mom."

"All is as it should be, then."

"Yes. All is as it should be." I stand. "I'd like to meditate on what you've told to me." My angel bows and disappears from view. I sit on the floor and take deep concentrated breaths until I enter the light once more.

Chapter Six

With each new day, new opportunities to learn are revealed.

Today, three new arrivals from the outside world found their way to our door. As with all newcomers, once they have been questioned by our military body, they are turned over to the medical staff, examined and processed. I take it upon myself, as I do with all new arrivals, to introduce myself. As I walk through the hospital doors I see a small, pale man, thin, frail even, sitting on a stool as mom draws blood from his arm.

I learn that his name is Dieter and that he calls himself a physicist. I learn that he came from another land, far away, across an ocean, many years ago. His English is perfect, but his accent thick. It is hard for me to picture other lands – he is my only exposure to the fact other cultures and languages exist.

After a short conversation he makes an astute observation.

"You understand more than your years would suggest," he announces, flinching as mom administers a vaccine to his left shoulder, a preventative measure we continue to practice in fear of the plague that killed so many following the bombs.

"I might say the same of you, if you weren't so old," I tease. His eyes widen and in studying them, a knowledge that extends far beyond the material *now*, reveals itself to me.

He laughs and rubs his shoulder. Looking up to mom he smiles. "Thank you very much."

"You're very welcome." She smiles back at him. "Your wife and son are waiting for you in the mess hall. Would you like me to take you to them?"

"Could I have a moment with your son?" He turns back to face me, his eyes squinting. "I think we have many things to discuss." He pulls down the short sleeve of his shirt and stands.

"I would like that," I agree. Looking to my mom, I ask, "Could you let his family know?"

She nods and winks at me. I watch Dieter eye her up as she leaves the doctor's office. Mom is a beautiful woman. Her big eyes and long lashes have captured the attention of every single man on the base at one time or another, and some women, but mom turns them all down. Her dedication to my studies and now her own, under Doctor Bren, have left her precious little time to pursue a personal life.

I urge Dieter to sit once more.

"From what your mother tells me, you must vibrate at an accelerated level."

"I, *vibrate?*"

"Yes. Well, we *all* vibrate. *Everything* vibrates, just at different frequencies." He crosses one leg over the other and places his folded hands upon his knee.

"That's an interesting statement. Enlighten me."

"Oh, I'm rather certain I could not *enlighten* one so far along the path as you." The wooden stool lets out a squeak as he leans back. "Tell me, what method do you use?"

"What do you mean I *vibrate?* That *everything* vibrates?"

"Forgive me. It's a theory that infinitesimally small vibrating strings pervade the universe, their different frequencies the very building blocks of all matter and energy in existence."

"O-kay." I say drawing out my response.

"And you, my friend, I can only imagine are approaching that moment, where it all comes together, where the quantum world is finally realized in this world. Perhaps you have already?"

"Who *are* you?" I ask fighting back a smile, realizing I'm in a conversation I may never understand.

"I am a quantum physicist." He leans forward on his stool and plants both feet on the ground. "I came to your country to teach the young scientists here, before the bombs fell." He looks up, raising his palms to the ceiling. "Since then I have travelled many years to find myself here. Yet no one I have met in all these years has expressed any interest in discussing with me the quantum world."

"Are you suggesting that you've found that person in *me?*" I must look incredulous at the implication.

"Yes."

"Why?"

"Your mother has told me you are a spiritual teacher here. She's told me you teach a form of meditation to your students and that you have been practicing since you were just a boy."

"Okay. And that makes me a scientist?"

"You are too modest." He wags a finger at me. "I have studied the effects of meditation on hundreds of people in congruence with my more 'scientific' research involving quantum physics, and have found similarities that may change the way we view the spiritual and scientific." Dieter pauses, and leans back on the stool once more. "I think you walk the line between this world and that. What you call the spiritual plane, I call the quantum plane."

"What is the quantum plane?"

"The quantum plane, or quantum physics, is the science of the very small."

"And you think the spiritual and quantum are one and the same?"

"That is my thinking. If God controls the quantum outcome, then He will determine *everything* in the end."

"You believe in God?"

Dieter runs his thin fingers along the stubble of silver hair framing a massive bald spot. "Maybe I do. You see, nothing is for certain at the quantum level. Space-time, or the physical realm, is ruled by four measurable forces, but something is working outside of space-time on the quantum plane."

"I'm not seeing the connection."

"What I believe, is that through your meditative practices, you leave the physical plane and walk with *God* in the quantum world."

I find myself becoming more and more involved in his homily. "So you think where my consciousness goes in meditation, and your quantum world, are the same place?" Dieter nods. "Why?"

He smiles. "Strings," he says, rising off of the stool. "The subatomic particles that make up every atom in the universe, which vibrate like the strings on a guitar when strummed, disappear and reappear all the time. They are not static here, in our physical plane, and we, as solids, bound by our three dimensions, could never experience them."

"But what of the mind?" I pose, beginning to understand what this brilliant man was alluding to.

"The mind?"

"Yes, in my teachings the mind is the spirit, and the mind is all knowing. If I am, as you say, walking with *God* in the quantum plane, shouldn't *I* be able to experience those other dimensions?"

"Yes, right, and I believe you *are*, when you meditate, shedding your physical self."

"Incredible."

"Indeed." With that Dieter stretches his lower back, arching his torso outward. "I should go. It is late and my family will be waiting."

"Of course. Let's discuss this further, another time. I am very interested in how your theory could be integrated with my own experiences."

"And I am very curious to discuss those experiences with you." He holds out a hand and I shake it. "Now, can you show me to my wife and boy?"

"Absolutely." I open the door and lead him down the hallway and into the cafeteria where his family greets him.

*****

Having grown up between worlds, living in the material plane while meditating in the spiritual, I have struggled with the approach I would take in order to pass the light of knowledge to others, as the two worlds seemed endlessly at odds with one another. But now that Dieter has introduced me to quantum physics, I am beginning to see how the two could co-exist.

*****

That night, hours after I'd gone to bed, a nightmare jolts me out of a deep sleep. My t-shirt and sheets are soaked in sweat.

My dreams and nightmares have carried warnings and premonitions in the past. If the jumbled images revealed to me tonight are any indication of a future event, I fear for myself and my community.

Chapter Seven

The following day the skies open up and release a torrential downpour. I invite mom to join me in the mess hall, pulling her away from her studies. For lunch we enjoy a slice of homemade bread and strawberry jam. It's a treat when the cooks prepare something fresh from our hydroponic gardens in the greenhouse. I watch as mom's face takes on an air of serenity. She chews each bite slowly, savoring the flavors.

She catches me smiling at her and smiles back.

"It's really good," I admit, staring at the thinly spread jam coating the thick slab of moist bread.

"You know what, Leif?" She looks at the piece of bread, turning it in her hands. "The last time I had strawberry jam was when I lived in the bunker, with my witches."

Mom and her witches. This was a recurring conversation between us. When I was a child they seemed more like a fairytale, a bedtime story. But then again, much of what she had taught me over the years was wisdom passed on from her witches. I still remember the first lesson, the pendulum. How empowered the exercise made me feel. That my thoughts alone could control the spinning of a weight at the end of a string was all at once magical and yet visceral. The idea that a thought was not contained in my head, but rather could be projected onto something real. The butterflies flutter in my stomach at the memory.

"Leif, I'd like to take you to see my witches, and I feel like they deserve to see you too, to *know* you."

"I would *love* to meet them." These women were so influential in my life, integral in my survival and in my teachings: Beth, Sally, Jenny and Carol. My chest stirs with excitement.

"Because, Leif, we wouldn't have made it here if it weren't for them," she continues, "and frankly, I've wanted to see them for a very long time."

"Of course," I lay a hand on hers. "Mom, let's go there."

She smiles up at me. I have towered over her since I was fourteen, when I experienced my biggest growth spurt. At eighteen I stand six feet, two inches.

"I'd also like to take you to your birthplace," she adds. "It's not far from the bunker."

"I'll talk to the Captain and have an escort take us there." I have no doubt the Captain will allow us this luxury. Though fuel is at a minimum, mom carries a certain respect among the officers and military personnel. Besides, one of the larger vehicles runs on electricity, of which we have an abundance.

*****

Once cleared, the Captain assigns soldiers to escort us on this day trip. It is an estimated two hours' travel to the house, and another hour to the bunker, allowing for a two hour return trip. We've been given an eight hour time allotment before we have to be back. That gives us roughly three hours to reminisce over mom's safe-house and sit with the women at the bunker and hope to bring them back with us.

The truck hurtles along at break-neck speed, weaving through a jungle of abandoned vehicles. It is an eerie thing, so many vehicles that had just stopped mid-journey; their occupants must have walked on to their deaths. I lean back in my seat, turning away from the window as I imagine entire families dying in this terrible aftermath. Mothers watching helplessly as their children give in to the ash and heat. Such scenes would have played out countless times the world over. A tear slips down my cheek and I wipe it away.

"Left here!" Mom calls from the front passenger seat. She reaches back to take my hand. I don't need to be an empath to sense we're close. We pull over slowly to the right at the top of a hill. Nothing indicates that there was ever a house here except the rusted cars and trucks that line the pot-marked driveway. Having burned down in a fire mom had set some eighteen years earlier, what remains of the house where she, my father and their friends had sought refuge, is only a hole in the ground where the foundation used to be. What timber that could be salvaged has been, and even the bricks and metal have been pilfered for some use. God only knows how anyone off our base existed for any length of time. I remember something the Sergeant told me once, about people, about how resilient our species is, and how driven we are to survive.

Mom walks down a slope in the yard approaching a pond. Her strides are long and determined. She is marching towards a memory. Behind the pond, which I'd been told was once a pool, she falls to her knees, her hands cradling her face. Then she bends further and touches her forehead to the earth.

KC walks past me, gesturing to his men and nodding at me. I nod back. As the soldiers rush past me to secure the perimeter I feel a sudden connection to the place where I was conceived and born. I imagine that the woods behind the house are green and alive and the fields stand high with corn stalks. The house towers above me, a massive brick structure. A gift from a memory of another life, my father's life before the end came. In reality, the forest now is spotted with only the strongest trunks - those with the deepest roots. They are not many and are black and bare. The fields to my right and behind me cultivate only dust now.

My attention again focuses on mom's sadness. I go and kneel beside her.

She looks up, wiping tears away. In her hand I see a bracelet. "This was Caroline's," she starts, holding the silver item up to me. "There's nothing else left of them."

This is where she had found her friends Sidney and Caroline after fleeing the fire. This is where Earl had ended their lives. Nothing remains but the bracelet now. But that is enough.

"She would want you to have it," I tell her.

Mom's bottom lip turns down and her chin trembles. "Do you think so?" Her teeth chatter. "Do you *know* so, Leif?"

I wrap my hands around hers and squeeze tight. "They are at peace now, Mom."

We walk the perimeter of the yard and even manage the trail back to a small cabin behind the house. The walk takes five minutes and we pass several grave markers. They rest beside a river bed, now dry and without purpose. She kneels down at each, placing a hand on the mounds one after another, whispering something inaudible. We spend a long moment at my father's grave, or what she remembers to be my father's grave. I find the sensation of being so close to the skeletal remains of my past life upsetting, and I move a few steps beyond the depression.

Then, a few seconds later into our walk, mom stops short in front of a branch connected to a thick trunk with a tattered rope tied to it. The rope has a noose at the end, like the ones we use at the base to hang criminals.

Mom's hands fly up to her mouth and a whimper slips through. I approach her and place my hands on her shoulders.

"What is it, Mom?"

Her head shakes. "Seth." The name materializes from a squeak at the back of her throat. Tears come next and I pull her into me and hug her hard.

After a time I release her and she smiles sadly up at me. "This is why we burned the house," she starts, pointing up at the gallows. "Earl had no right to do this… that bastard… cowardly bastard."

Mom approaches the noose and asks me to pull it down. I need to jump, but I get a grip and tear it down, the branch snapping away from the trunk. As we continue to move towards the shed, a sharp pain strikes me in my thigh. It's unlike anything I've felt before.

"Are you okay, Leif?" Mom asks, watching as my hands automatically grasp my thigh and the breath leaves me. The pain lasts only a moment, and I shake my head.

"I'm okay. Just a muscle spasm, I guess." I shake my leg, wondering at the intensity of the pain, and continue walking.

At the shed we come upon a strange sight. One that none after mom's Apocalypse has witnessed in the natural world. There is a single flower poking through the battered earth. Plants grew because we grew them, period, not in the wild. Not anymore. Mom bends toward the strange flower. She looks up at me and smiles. "It's Jake," she tells me. "This is where he died. He died protecting your father." Her head falls back to the flower and she inhales its scent.

"This is incredible, right?" I say. "This doesn't happen."

"No." Mom stands and crossing her arm, smiles. "No, it doesn't."

I lean in to smell the flower. I touch the earth surrounding the plant and it is moist. "Should we take it with us?"

"No." She doesn't miss a beat.

I rise and nod in approval, amazed at the mystery of the thing. We turn and head back to the Hummer. In my peripheral I see a soldier on either side of us, shadowing our movements, ever aware of their surroundings.

Chapter Eight

The drive from my father's family home to mom's safe-house gives me an hour to contemplate the feelings I pulled from the experience. Mom's stories became more real after visiting the place where my father once lived, the home my grandfather built, which had housed mom and thirteen of her peers for nearly two years after the bombs. I feel connected to my past both physically and spiritually. I meditate on the place, seated in the back of the Hummer, memories that are not my own race through my mind's eye.

I awaken from my trance as the doors to the vehicle are pushed open. The sun is falling behind the horizon, elongating the shadows of a distant forest. I step out of the Hummer and stretch. Mom walks toward a structure just a few feet ahead of us.

A veranda overlooks a large yard. A burnt out structure, long since reduced to its footings, lay behind it. Mom approaches the veranda with trepidation. I can tell that she is frightened of what she might find.

She pulls at a trapdoor at the base of the veranda and seems surprised when it opens. She looks back at me with her mouth open and eyes wide. I approach. Taking the door from her I swing it open, revealing a dark pit below.

"Bethany?!" She whispers into the abyss. "Jenny? Carol? Sally?!" There is no reply. Mom looks up at me and stands. "I need to go down there."

I wave over one of the corporals and ask for his flashlight. "I'm coming with you." She wraps a hand around my forearm and I switch on the flashlight.

"Can you guys wait for us up here?" I ask KC as he joins us.

"You're sure, Leif?" His eyes dart to the cluster of dead trees just a few yards north of us.

I look to her and she nods. "No one knew about this place."

"We're sure." I lay a hand on his shoulder and step onto the ladder. Mom follows.

Reaching the bottom I feel the grit of dirt under my soles. I turn with the light and shine it down a long narrow passage. The place smells damp.

"Beth?!" Mom calls out again. And again she looks up at me, her forehead creased.

"Maybe they've stepped out. We could wait for them."

She shakes her head and arm in arm we move through the darkened tunnel, and into a larger room.

Mom takes the flashlight from me and shines it frantically about the barrel shaped interior.

"Where *is* everyone?"

"Could they have moved on?"

She throws open cupboards and drawers. "Why would they leave? Look at this! There is still food here." She opens another trapdoor and climbs down a set of stairs.

"Wait! Mom!" I follow.

When I reach the basement of the shelter I stand in awe of the collection of canned and boxed goods. Everything from matches to jerky; dried fruit and juice boxes stacked in neat piles set on metal shelves; baby formula and diapers and toilet paper. All in what seems like a temperature controlled dry room.

"Why would anyone leave this place?" She ignites an oil lamp that hangs from the low ceiling. "I don't understand." She runs her hands along the jars and boxes.

"What would you like to do?" I ask, wondering if we ought to stay for a night and wait them out.

She nods as if reading my mind. "Let's stay a night or two. We can send the others home if they'd like to get back."

"They won't leave us here alone, Mom. You know that."

"I guess I do. But they might not let us stay."

"I'll talk to them. There's more than enough room down here for everyone." We reach the main floor of the bunker and close the door to the dry storage.

"Maybe I could clean it up a bit." She studies the place, her eyes flinching as they fall on objects and items of clothing.

"Everything okay, Mom?"

"No." She stares at the kitchen table. A Ouija board sits alone in the center. She shines the light over to a couch and coffee table adjacent the kitchen, where a deck of illustrated cards is laid out in a circular pattern. I watch the memories play out on her face, her eyes darting from one scene to the next. I approach her and gently lay a hand on her back.

"Can you tell me what's wrong?"

She bends down to pick up a piece of paper from the coffee table. "The horoscope…" Her voice trails off.

"Is this *my* horoscope? The one that Jenny researched for you?" I ask excitedly.

With vacant eyes she looks up at me, handing me a piece of paper. I take it from her and look it over. Flipping it in my hands, I notice nothing is written on it. I walk closer to the table and pick up the other sheets. All are blank.

"Did she not write down the information?" A shiver works its way up my spine.

"Of course, she did." Doubt creeps into her eyes as she pans the room for more details.

"Okay. Well, this must not be it then. Where would it be?"

"No, that's it."

"How can you be sure?"

"The corners." I study the corners of the paper more closely. They are turned in. "I turned them myself, to keep them together, but, that was long before I ever left here." She starts to pace between the kitchen and the living area. "I told you, we left abruptly. I packed our gear when the message came from your Blank Man, and left."

I remember the story. I sit on the armrest of the couch and watch her work through her memories.

"Ask him a question for me, Leif." She turns to me. "Ask him if they were *real*."

"Real? You think they didn't actually exist?"

"Once, yes." She studies her hands, her fingers interlocking.

"But not anymore?"

"Not even while I was here." Her head shakes slowly.

"Ghosts?"

"Yes." She stares straight ahead.

A moment passes, I focus on the question, not even sure I should relay the information Blank Man gives me to mom, who seems to be in shock. Still, when the answer is offered, I know that she must know.

"He says yes." I nod. "They were *earth bound* spirits. Free-spirits."

I watch as she shivers, and catch her as she loses her balance, placing her on the couch and sitting next to her.

"He's telling me that just weeks after the bombs fell, they succumbed to a virus just beyond the property line. In the woods to the north."

"The strain that killed so many?"

"Yes, the same." I answer. "But they'd made a pact. They would return. Free-spirits are powerful entities, living in this plane and that. They know they have passed, but are determined to see a thing through."

Suddenly I see the women in my mind's eye, a gift from Blank Man: the four witches, bathed in light. One chubby and kind, one with jet black hair and olive skin, another pale white and thin, and lastly, the one named Beth. She out-shines them all, and as they smile at me they turn, and walk out of sight, and into the light.

I look to my mom to tell her what I'd seen and notice a tear balancing on her chin.

"I saw them, Leif. Did you see them?" She wipes her face.

"Yes."

"Weren't they beautiful?"

"Yes, Mom."

"Thank him for me will you? Your Blank Man. That meant more to me…" I hug her and let her cry until the men that have accompanied us on this pilgrimage interrupt our moment with a shout down the tunnel.

"We've got company, Leif!" calls KC. "We need to get moving!"

"Be out in a moment!"

Mom pulls back from me and smiles, wiping her face. Then carefully she holds my face in her hands. "I'm so very glad you had the chance to meet them, Leif. They would be so proud."

I gently wrap my hands around her wrists and, smiling lead her out of the bunker to find the soldiers kneeling beside the trapdoor, rifles drawn.

"Get low." KC motions with his hand.

"What is it?" I whisper.

"Not sure. We heard rustling in the woods."

It is dark out. More time has passed in the bunker than I realized. The night sky is ominous, a great cloud blotting out the full moon. Then we see it, a pack of dogs emerging from the forest to the north, some one hundred yards from our position.

"Look at that," says one of the soldiers. "I've never seen so many at once."

The pack has picked up our scent, and curiously approaches.

"Let's make our way back to the vehicle," KC orders in a whisper. "No sudden movements. Just follow me."

We pick ourselves up and, crouching, make slow deliberate steps towards the waiting Hummer. The pack picks up its pace and breaks into a run.

"Move!" shouts KC. "Cover us!" He grabs my mother's arm and pulls her beside him. I follow, flanking left. It's obvious the dogs will overtake us before we make the Hummer. Three of the soldiers stop and turn to face the starving dogs, steadying themselves on one knee. Then their rifles shatter the silence, I hear the dogs whimper as they fall to the hail of bullets.

Once safely inside, KC slams the door behind us and fires his weapon at the beasts. I feel terrible the dogs were being gunned down like this, but they were starving and would not have hesitated to rip us to pieces.

As we look on, one solider trips as he runs backwards, expertly targeting one after another of the hungry dogs. Hitting the ground hard, his rifle fires into the night sky. KC and another solider rush to his side but not before one of the dogs has his ankle in its mouth. Then another is on top of him, tearing at his thigh. KC picks them off one by one with his rifle, managing to drag the man to the safety of the Hummer.

We shift to one side of the vehicle and assist in placing the wounded man on the folded seats. Mom goes right to work examining the wounds.

"Is he alright?" KC asks.

"He'll be fine," She tells us. "You'll be fine," she repeats to the wounded soldier.

I turn to KC. "There's a lot of food and accessories in that bunker."

"We should get Devin back to the hospital now," Mom insists.

KC nods. "We've mapped out the trip, so we can come back anytime to retrieve everything." He turns in his seat and gives the order to head back to base.

The Hummer speeds off.

Chapter Nine

A week following the field trip, the Sergeant and I sit in the cafeteria after Father Henderson's Sunday service, ready to assist in rearranging the tables and chairs to once again resemble a mess hall.

The Sergeant and I have a strange relationship. Mom avoids him, and has since I was nine. I'd noticed sadness in him, reflected in his aura when I would talk to him about her. But I always felt drawn to him, as a role model and the face of leadership on the base.

I shift in my seat as I watch what represents close to ninety percent of our residents shuffle into the hallway, discussing the sermon excitedly. The sermon dealt with what was the Holy Land; its purpose and its destiny. Its history is what most intrigues me: a violent, passionate history that spanned its entire existence.

"I can't imagine putting such stock in a *place*, in property," I say, the Sergeant looks to me, his eyes narrowing. "I mean; to attribute such worth to a *thing*."

"I would *die* for this place," he retorts. His wife lays a hand on his shoulder and joins the mass exodus. "Imagine our lives if we didn't have all of this."

"Point taken."

I had read extensive literature on the great and many religions of the world stored in the library's computer archives. I'd spoken at length with Father Henderson on religion, and its historical hold on humanity. From a very young age I found myself drawn to the subject and to the concept of possession.

"You know, Leif, what you speak about often reminds me of what the Grimm Reaper preached to the world before he ended it. We have records of his web logs and news articles. He demanded an end to organized religion and governments. He saw possessions as the devil's influence."

"Even the devil will quote scripture if it serves him."

Chapter Ten

My interest in my father's past tugs at my curiosity as I sit at a computer station in the library, considering his immoral act against his friend. I understand destiny, and so realize that there was more at work than just a paranoid mind acting irrationally.

Connor could see future events, and would unconsciously prepare graves behind my father's house, while in a trancelike state. But what really connected me to Connor was that he could *see* my angel.

These characters from mom's past were becoming more and more connected as I related the information: from the Reaper, to the flags, to the angel, to Connor, and to my father, and now, *me*.

I summon Blank Man. He appears before me as the dark figure I have come to trust, a *halo* of white light outlining his frame.

"Tell me about Connor," I ask.

"Connor was gifted with second sight. He found his gift to be a burden, but before his end came, he was given clarity, and so saw his own end."

"The flags," I interjected.

"Yes, the flags, and your father. Connor was gifted the future far beyond his own, and his friends. He saw *you*, Leif. He saw you take up your father's destiny, and so accepted his own, allowing his death at the hands of the flags, so that a future where you would complete the task he knew your father would forsake could be realized."

A sick feeling attacks my abdomen. "If my father could betray a friend, does that mean I may betray someone? I *am* my father, after all."

"You are and you are not, Leif. You are yourself, with your father's experiences to draw from. Most cannot draw from the experiences of their past lives, but you have that power."

"Why do you hold so much back? Why have you not told me this part of the story before?"

"It has no bearing on your destiny, but now that you have asked, and I have told you, you must be made aware. Begin the process of meditation." I cross my legs and place my hands on my knees, close my eyes and enter into the light. "Good, now see your father. Approach him and speak to him. He will offer you only truth."

I find my father in the light. He is young: my age. He smiles and I see myself in him. He is me. It is a difficult concept to grasp, but the closer we get to one another, the more his truth is revealed to me. I feel anxious at first, and then terribly sad, then strangely happy, and then numb. Then I feel anger, and jealousy and hate. Next I feel betrayal, then guilt and pain. Then there is light, and warmth and a sense of peace. All these emotions offer a story, and the story was deeply upsetting. But I understand it like I'd lived it. I understand my father.

"Do not make the same mistakes your father made."

As I ease out of my meditative state, I open my eyes and see Tina, the librarian, kneeling next to me with a glass of water in hand.

"Leif?" she asks. "Are you alright, honey?"

I smile, blink hard and unwrap my legs. "I am, Tina. Thank you." I take the water. "Have I been here long?"

Everyone on the base was used to my meditative 'moments' now, as they often struck me in odd, and unusual places.

"Not sure. I saw you walk in an hour ago, but how long you've been meditating, I couldn't say."

"Just an hour, then?" I stand and shake out my legs, allowing the blood to return to my feet.

"Yes."

Perfect, I was to meet mom for dinner in a few minutes. I thank Tina for the water and head for the mess hall.

*****

"I have something for you, Leif." Mom looks up from her plate. She seems

49

preoccupied, moving the mashed potatoes around with her fork. "It's one of my only possessions and it's something your father wrote just before he died."

This was exciting: a physical relic from the past. Something my father had touched - something he'd written.

"You know how your father died?"

I nod.

"I didn't want to tell you."

"Of course, I know you don't tell a kid his dad killed himself." I lay a gentle hand on her arm.

"I was afraid one day you'd learn the truth. Does your *Blank Man* have to tell you everything?"

"There is a truth you wanted to know once."

She stares for a minute at me and shakes her head. "Once. Just for a fleeting moment."

"Okay, Mom," I say, letting it go. "Now where is this letter?"

She produces the paper from her pocket.

"I keep it with me at all times. So I never forget." She hands me the fragile artifact and I carefully unfold it on the cafeteria table. There are two pieces of lined paper with two distinctly different sets of handwriting. I look at Mom, who is watching me. I smile widely, my heart in my throat. The idea that Dad had left something tangible behind is exhilarating. Though I'd met him in my meditation and spoken to him and shared his experiences and emotions, this is something I could touch, and hold in my hands.

I hesitate, closing my eyes and inhaling deeply. I read the neatly handwritten verse first.

I know now that a single action can put in motion a series of repercussions. Should that action be positive, the repercussions are rewarding, but when that action is negative, so too are the events to follow. A single action can change you forever. Sometimes, if the deed is large enough, if the intent evil enough, the results can be disastrous.

I look at her again and can't believe what I've read. It's a suicide note.

"Are you okay?" She brushes my cheek with the back of her hand.

"It's Dad making sense of everything." I say, the gravity of my father's decisions weighing now on my shoulders. "He's explaining his actions, but also reliving the whole Grimm Reaper scenario in this one paragraph."

"You are a smart man." Mom runs her hand up and down my arm. "Read on."

I slide the top verse to the side and read the page with the sloppy print.

Blank   Page,   Blank   Mind,   Blank   Brain,   Blank   man.
Blink   and   Blank   man   disappears,   blink   and   Blank   man   disappears.
Blink,   and   nobody   cares.   Blink   blinky,   blink   blinky,   blink   Bitch!
If   I   could,   I'd   blink,   if   only   I   could   blink.   I'd   be   Blinky,   blinking.
Blank man would disappear.

After the fourth pairing on the first line I look back to her and mouth the words, *Blank Man*. She nods.

I read on. Once finished I read it again and again and again. The cryptic poem is filled with angst, but also carries a message of enlightenment with it.

To achieve a *blank mind* is to allow no thoughts, as in meditation allowing the participant to enter the light.

But the fact that he uses *Blank Man* spurs a question to Mom.

"Did Dad call his angel Blank Man?"

"No, that's all you. Joel didn't call him anything. He didn't have a name for him. Angel is about the only thing I ever heard him call it in his sleep."

"I'd like to copy it down, Mom. I want to go over it again."

"It's yours now, Leif. Do with it what you wish. I've held onto it long enough."

*****

Tonight another nightmare forces me from my sleep. My muscles are tense; I sit up, fighting to remember its message. Fear for one, fear of loss, fear of the unknown. These dreams are becoming more and more ominous. They are warnings. Something is coming, something sinister.

Chapter Eleven

Mary came to me in a dream. That was the first time I saw her, but in my dream she was leaving me.

The second time I met Mary was in the physical world. She, along with a half dozen other survivors, were escorted into the central parade grounds, then one by one marched into the infirmary. There they were disrobed and given showers and shots from the medical staff while mom and Doctor Bren supervised.

She was beautiful, even after going months, or maybe years, without a bath. Her hair was filthy, matted and pressed against her head, and her lips unnaturally pouty against her thin, malnourished face. As I stood beside the growing crowd that watched this new group shuffle into our lives her gaze met mine, and I was under her spell.

I make it a point to meet all new arrivals, to welcome them and explain our set-up. I make sure Mary is alone when I approach her in the mess hall. I watch as she cleans the last of her dinner off the plate.

"Hello." I say as I sit across from her.

"Hi." She seems distracted, pressing her finger against the plate, picking up the crumbs of bread and cheese.

My eyes had not deceived me earlier. She *is* beautiful. Even with her hair shaved to the scalp, as was the practice with new arrivals, her face seemed angelic. She catches me staring again, and I look away, red-faced.

"I saw you when we got here," she says shyly.

"Yes," I say clumsily. "It's always a big deal when the soldiers find new people."

"*We* found *them*," she insists, a smile playing across her flawless face.

I find myself smiling back. "However it happened, I'm very happy to have you here."

"I've never known anything like this place." She looks around the mess hall and inhales deeply. "Is this Heaven?"

I laugh aloud but stop myself. "I'm sorry," I say, watching her brows meet in the middle and her smile fade.

"It was a stupid question, I know, but if you knew how we've lived…" Her hands fly up to hide her face. Her body jerks violently as she sobs.

I stand and round the table, seating myself next to her, and carefully place a hand on her shoulder. She jumps and shifts back in her seat. I remove my hand quickly, realizing I've startled her.

"I'm so sorry," I whisper, careful not to upset her further.

"No, I'm sorry, I didn't – I'm sorry." Her head shakes as she lowers her hands, wiping away the tears.

"Don't be." I feel uneasy now. This isn't at all how I'd pictured this meeting going.

"Look, I've never been touched by anyone but my parents."

"I understand, really, you don't have to explain."

"You seem like a nice boy," she begins. "I – I'm just a little shaky. It's kind of a lot to take in, being here: new people and everything."

"I get it, I do. I'm sorry if I was too forward."

A smile twitches at the corners of her mouth. "It's alright. Let's start over." She extends a thin hand, lined with delicate veins. "I'm Mary Gardener."

"Leif," I tell her, feeling silly having not introduced myself immediately.

"Could you stay and talk, Leif?"

"If that's what you'd like." I feel giddy at the request.

"Please." She closes her eyes and seems suddenly tired. I wonder what this girl has had to endure. "It's been a little overwhelming for me. The others are catching up on their sleep, so I took the opportunity to just be alone for a while. I guess when you've spent so much time with the same people… well, I love them, but it's nice to have a break."

"Are you related to any of them?" I secretly pray she was not romantically linked to one of the younger men.

"One of the women is my mother, and the older man a sort of step-father to me. One of the boys is a cousin and another woman an aunt. The smallest of the boys we picked up a few months ago."

"How old are you, if you don't mind?"

"How old? I don't even really know for sure. We tried to keep track of the weeks and months and years, but gave up after the last of our journals was used up. That was a very long time ago."

"Do you remember how old you were in year one?"

"Year one?"

"Yes, the year of the bombs. We have a complete library of the weeks and months and years following, so if you knew your age then, I could tell you your age now."

"I was five when the bombs dropped," she says without hesitation. "What does that make me?"

"It's been about twenty years since that day. That makes you twenty five."

"Twenty years. I don't really know what that means. I'm not sure I ever did." It makes sense that someone who'd moved from place to place in search of food and shelter, with no semblance of structure, would have little use for concepts such as years or even months. Seasons yes, but months and weeks? The light of day would give way to the darkness and repeat. What else was there?

"Will you let me take you to see someone?"

She looks at me with wide eyes and I imagine she's sizing me up: friend or foe? I smile without thinking, studying her perfect features.

Mary nods and stands. I follow her lead and wave for her to join me as I walk towards the door of the cafeteria.

*****

Tina is dressed in her pressed army issue pant suit when we meet her at the library entrance. She takes her role at the base seriously, and works hard at keeping concise records of life after the Apocalypse. Tina came to the base from a northern city turned upside down after the bombs landed. When society failed and resources ran dry, she travelled alone, and was one of the first civilians to arrive at the base. From that point on she has kept the records.

"Leif, I was just closing up to get some dinner."

"Oh, that's okay, Tina. We can come back another time."

"No, don't be silly, you're welcome to use the library." She shifts her attention to Mary. "And is this one of the new arrivals?"

"Yes," I say proudly. "This is Mary." My new friend nods and smiles at Tina. Tina eyes me and a sly smile forms on her face.

"Listen, you're obviously here to talk to me. Come inside." She opens the door and I let Mary pass through first. I smile broadly, and Tina rubs my back knowingly. I wish Mary would pick up on my interest in her as quickly and effortlessly as Tina has.

"Has Leif told you about what it is I do here on the base, Mary?"

"He's told me some of what you do," she admits shyly.

"Come to my terminal and I'll show you the rest." Tina leads us to the desk where she spends much of her days. We gather behind her as she sits at the computer.

"I have kept records of this place in the time following the bombs," she explains. "But in addition to that, I have been recording Leif's life."

"*My* life?" I blurt, incredulous. "What, why?"

"Your mother never told you?" She turns to me, and my stunned expression is reflected in her bifocaled lenses. "Mary, you've made a very important friend in Leif."

I look at Mary and realize she has been staring at me. My face reddens and I smile at her awkwardly. I don't know if the stirring in my stomach comes from Tina's words or the intensity of Mary's gaze. It's a new feeling for me. Yes, I've noticed girls before, but the few women close to my age had become like sisters to me. This was new, exciting, and potentially devastating. It was more than mere physical attraction. There was a feeling in my chest that suddenly explained to me the expression 'heartbreak'.

Tina brings up a page of text on the screen and I read the title: *Leif. Years 1 – 10*. And then again as she scrolls down dozens of pages: *Leif. Years 11-18*.

"Leif is our moral and spiritual center here, and has been since he was just a child."

"I'm sorry, Mary, I didn't know." I feel she must think I'd brought her here to hear all about *me*. "Tina, what has mom told you?"

"Everything, Leif. She's told me everything."

"Why? Why would she do that?"

"She did it because she wanted a record of your life, so that one day your story and your words would reach others." She turns once more to face us both. "She did this for all of us, Leif."

I step back to sit on a chair a few feet behind me. Mary follows.

I knew her heart was in the right place, and that others could benefit from what I'd been talking about for years. My concern was personal. The ramifications were ego, and I had tried so long to avoid building one. With the release of something like this, would others get the wrong idea?

"I understand the purpose behind what you've done. I just have no interest in being *anyone's* center. If there is one thing I teach it's that meditation and spiritual realization happens within *you*, not through someone else. Please, Tina do me this one thing, and remove my name from the files. Let the words stand alone."

"Of course, Leif," she says. "I understand."

I reach out to her and she places her hands in mine. "Thank you."

My trip with Mary to the library had turned into something far different than I had imagined. I look up again and see she's looking right back, a renewed level of interest on her face, and a glow I could hopefully call something more than friendliness.

*****

I walk Mary to her room. Her mother and step-father are pacing about in the hall.

"Where were you?" her mom asks, rushing to meet us.

"Just at the library with Leif."

"Mrs. Gardner," I say.

"We were worried, Mary." Her eyes are red and swollen from crying.

"I'm very sorry. I had no intention of upsetting you," I apologize. "I just wanted Mary to know about the books."

"Leif, it's okay," Mary reassures me. "Mom, it's okay, I'm not even late for the Sergeant's tour."

"I know, I'm sorry." Her mother looks at me next. "I'm sorry, Leif, it's just, we've never been apart."

"It won't happen again without you knowing, Mrs. Gardner. I promise."

"Thanks, Leif." Mary brushes her hand against my arm. The sensation leaves goose-bumps in its wake. "I'll see you tomorrow."

"Yes, please," I say, barely aware of how silly I sound.

Mrs. Gardner walks her to her room, on the opposite side of the hall.

Mary's step-father walks toward me and lands a heavy hand on my shoulder.

"We're very grateful to be here," he starts. "Just know that we've been through a lot. You can't imagine." He stops himself, his head falling forward. Then he looks up at me again. "We're very grateful to be here."

I walk out of the family housing building and toward the hospital. A goofy smile plays out on my face as I dwell on Mary. The promise she would see me in the morning would make it difficult to sleep tonight. The morning could not come soon enough.

Chapter Twelve

Today is the day I discover what punishment Harry, Chris and Monty have been handed for their attack over a week earlier. I watch as an armed escort leads them to my meditation circle and nudges them to sit. They obey. None of them look up at me. They'd been held all this time in the stockade. So, sitting in on my meditation classes is to be their punishment. The irony and wisdom of the Captain's decision brings a smile to my face. I try not to take too much pleasure in their misery, but find it impossible to repress.

I use advanced yoga after our first round of meditation to further teach my oppressors a lesson, but am careful not to be cruel.

Warming down from the yoga I hold my pose and reflect on the night before. I feel awkward after Tina's surprise biography, but what I feel for Mary when I think on her is stranger still. I notice Mary in my peripheral, lingering just beyond the canopy of trees in the wooded corner of the base as the sun is just breaking the horizon. I ask my class to break and move to meet her.

"So, this is what you do with your days?" The smile on her face is genuine, and a little mocking. I like it.

My hands shoot into my pockets and my eyes fall to the ground. Her small top is too small I think, but would never bring it to her attention.

Mary touches my forearm. "Oh, Leif, I didn't mean it to embarrass you." A kind smile replaces the playful one of moments ago. My heart leaps at her touch.

"I'm not embarrassed," I say, pulling my hands out of my pockets. "Not about this anyway. I am a little embarrassed about what happened last night at the library."

"Don't be," she says, shaking her head.

"Please, Mary, I want you to know *me*." I pause, wondering what my next words will be and then they surface. "Not someone else's version, but the *real* me."

"Is this not the *real* you?" she asks turning to the group behind us.

"It is," I nod. "But there is another me, and I'd like to share him with you." The words just keep coming; I feel I've lost control of my tongue. "Would you be interested in knowing me?"

A silence that I know is only one to two seconds feels like an eternity as Mary's eyes find mine and she answers.

"Yes." Her face ignites in white light as she moves to the right, stepping out of my shadow. "I would like that."

A buzzing in my chest erupts.

"Dinner?" I manage.

"Yes. Mess hall?"

"Yes." I answer. "Six?" I turn towards the group, reluctant for the first time I can remember to continue meditating.

Chapter Thirteen

The following week, Mary and I can't seem to spend enough time with one another. I encourage her to sit in on my meditation classes, and even to accompany me in my personal meditation. Mary is a quick study. She takes to the physical aspects of Yoga very quickly, allowing the mental facet of each session to fall in line. She is showing great promise in commanding her mind and body.

"I'm chasing the light," she says, patting her forehead with a hand-towel after an intensive mid-day class.

I laugh. 'Chasing the light' is Mary's new expression: a satirical description of her journey to enlightenment. She's very witty, which I have grown to appreciate.

"I think that's what we'll call your biography," I tell her. "'Chasing the Light: The Mary Gardener Story.'" She smiles back and whips the towel in my direction.

"Maybe I'll have a place in *your* story," she suggests, closing in on me. "But not my own." She is suddenly standing so close that the heat from her body feels as though it's enveloping me. I move backwards, and she follows, pinning me gently against the wall. My heels hit the steel with a bang, the sound startling us both.

"It was just the heels of my shoes," I blurt awkwardly. I'm not sure where to place my hands.

She pulls back. "Good, I'm glad you didn't bump your head." She was blushing now. Had I ruined a moment? She looks at the ground.

I know this is it, and I have to seize the moment. As if possessed, I place a finger under her chin and lift her face to mine. I feel my heart race. I lean toward Mary and our lips lock in a long, soft kiss.

Whistles and nervous laughter from the class enter my head like echoes, pulling me out of the moment.

"I'm sorry," I say, surprising myself once again. Mary's eyes pop open and her head jerks back.

"You are?" she whispers, her brows pushing up the middle of her forehead.

"No." I shake my head. "No, I don't know why I said that."

Mary smiles and takes my face in both hands, pulling me toward her. We kiss for a long time, eventually sitting on a bench.

Mary pulls back an inch or two and holds my face in her hands. She looks at me as if to say *I trust you*. I smile and my fingers find the line of her cheek bones and jaw. I trace them to her chin.

"Thank you for wanting this," she says, but I'm not sure what she means.

"I do," I assure her, regardless of the meaning.

"So do I."

We move toward each other again wrapping our arms around one other. Mary climbs on top of me, straddling me, and squeezes. I squeeze back.

After a time we stand. The class has dismissed themselves. I take her hand and we walk around the base. We say nothing. I find it difficult to quiet my mind. I want to kiss Mary again but feel suddenly shy. I want to tell her things, things that will make her smile and laugh and love me. Love me?

Is it so easy to fall in love? Why shouldn't it be? Why would it take any time at all?

Was I in love?

Chapter Fourteen

Tina has come to every meditation and assembly I've ever called, and now I knew why. She had been writing my biography.

"It's not just your words, Leif, that I'm capturing. It's your story," she explains, seated across from me in the empty cafeteria. It's three o'clock in the morning. I couldn't sleep and ran into Tina while walking the compound. I look up at her, putting aside the notes she had scribbled over the past 17 years. "And you've transferred all of these to your computer?"

Tina nods. "I'll print and bind them in a day."

I push the stack of paper back to her, having read my biography over the course of the last two nights. My neck feels tight and I rub it hard with my palm.

"Then why not tell the whole story, Tina?" I suggest. "Mom told you everything, you said." She nods again. "Then you know my story goes far beyond my years in this body. "

"What are you saying, Leif?"

"Tell my father's story as well. To tell only mine makes the story incomplete."

"How could I tell your father's story with any accuracy? Your mother knows her side only…"

I cut her off. "I know it intimately. You can listen as I meditate on my father's life and record everything I say."

"You can do that?"

"Yes."

"When did you want to start?"

"Right now," I say and she rises out of her chair. We walk quickly out of the mess hall and to the library where I have the privacy to recite the whole story.

*****

The work Tina and I had managed in the night was exhausting. I lament on the night before. Living my father's experiences, my past life, was devastating. We did get through it all though, and since Tina and mom had conspired to write my story, I felt it only right to be completely honest, offering the whole story from start to finish. Tina said she would interview mom next in an effort to collect a more detailed telling of when, eighteen years ago, she and I made our way here, to the safety of the base. That way she would have a complete tale up to the present day, to be added to as necessary.

So now Tina would have three books. Labeled as such: Book I A.A., book II A.A, Book III A.A.

*****

Another nightmare leaves me at a loss tonight. Another warning of what will come to pass, another riddle to decode. The continuous assault on my subconscious by these distorted images and the emotions they carry with them have been hard on my nerves. I breath in, hold and release. I continue this practice until I settle down.

I haven't brought up these premonitions, if that's what they are, with my angel, but Blank Man has not approached me about them either. Though their imagery is muddied, their purpose seems clear. We are approaching an end that will not come quietly.

Chapter Fifteen

At dinner, Dieter sits next to Mary and across from me, his tray of food landing softly on the steel table. He is smiling as only Dieter does. His mouth, though sparsely populated with teeth, is never anyone's focus. His eyes shine brightly, projecting an extraordinary wisdom. I feel his excitement. It has been only two weeks since his arrival, but I already feel as though he will become a close friend. I am anxious to speak more with him, and I am sensing he feels the same.

"Hello, Leif." He turns to Mary. "And hello, beautiful Mary." She blushes, smiling. I wink in her direction and turn back to Dieter.

"How are you, Dieter?" I smile at him, my eyes darting between him and Mary.

"I wanted to continue our conversation," he says sheepishly. "I know that I talk above people on this subject – I told my wife about you and she thought maybe I was too forward."

"Well, you definitely had me at a disadvantage. But I caught the gist of it."

"Well, I wanted to just clear the air. I know we haven't had much contact since I got here, but getting settled seems to have taken more time than expected. You know, they have me working with the solar panels and windmills."

"I'm glad you've found something. We try to give people work that matches their skills, but pretty sure no one is hiding a physics lab on the base."

We share a laugh.

"This is fine for me." His hands wave frantically in front of him. "I've always loved sustainable power technologies. But, I did want to sit with you again and answer any question you might have since our last discussion."

"Yes, there are likely many more than I can think to ask on the spot, but maybe you could catch Mary up on our conversation." I ask as much for Mary's sake as my own.

"Certainly." He shifts in his seat to face her.

"I was five the last time I went to school," Mary admits. "My mom taught me things from books that we found as we moved from place to place, and I learned to read and write, but I wouldn't waste your time on me."

"It is never a waste to offer an education to someone willing to accept it." Dieter moves his tray of greens and bread to his right.

Mary nods and sits at attention. He takes up a roll in his hand and raises it over his head.

"What happens when I release this piece of bread?" he asks her.

Mary looks to me and then back to Dieter. "It will fall."

"Right, it will fall, but, why?"

"Gravity?"

"Yeah! Right again, Mary! Gravity is one of the four forces we can directly experience. The planet was created because of gravity, the solar system was pulled together by the gravity of the sun, and our galaxy was formed by the gravity of the black hole that sits in the centre. Everything we see is affected by gravity."

"Okay, I understand that," Mary says with a growing confidence.

"Good, Mary, so while classical physics describes the universe around us, or the very big, a physicist cannot apply it to the very small, the quantum world."

"Now I'm lost," Mary smiles. I laugh at her candor.

"Imagine something smaller than the smallest thing you can see with your eyes, Mary," continues Dieter, undeterred. "Now, imagine something a million times smaller."

Mary leans back in her seat at the thought, shaking her head. "I can't."

"And you are not alone. Few could. Allow me to take you to the hospital research area. They have a microscope there that is very powerful."

"Leif?" Mary looks for my approval.

I shrug. "I'd like to see where he's going with this too." I stand and we march out of the mess hall, Dieter stuffing the roll in his mouth.

Upon arriving at the hospital, Mary and I wait outside the research lab while Dieter speaks with Doctor Bren about using his microscope for a presentation. I watch as the doctor nods and waves us into the room.

Inside, Dieter places a flat glass panel with a red spot on it under the microscope's eye. "Mary, please, come and see what I mean." He points at his eye and then at the scope urging Mary to stare into the eye-piece. She bends over the microscope and places one eye on the scope. I watch as her mouth opens and a smile grows across her face.

"It is blood," says Dieter, nodding my way, his arms crossed. "Thousands of times bigger than you see with your own eyes."

Mary looks up and her eyes turn to Dieter. "But it doesn't even look like blood." Her head falls back to the microscope.

"No, so you can see how something that defines a universe we can see with our own eyes, the macroscopic, would have trouble defining a world as small as the one you are witnessing now, the microscopic."

"Could I see, Mary?" I ask, walking toward her. She nods and I lean in for a look. This must have been what Father Henderson meant when he said he'd *'found God'* in the intelligent design of all things, before he left his career as a biologist.

What I see in no way represents a drop of blood in my experience. It's not a liquid, but broken down into dozens of puck-like forms, opening my eyes to just how complex the physical world really is.

"That's incredible," I whisper.

"And that is not even close to what I was able to see when I had my own laboratory. So, you start to see that the very small make up the very big and this world of the very small is very different than what you see with your own eyes."

"It's amazing," says Mary, now holding my arm.

"It is that." Dieter takes a breath. "This is why quantum physics was realized. When you go another step, you see atoms, and then the subatomic particles, like hadrons and quarks."

I fear Dieter is starting to talk beyond his audience again and jump in. "But the strings you told me about? You can't see those?"

"No, sadly," answers Dieter. "These will remain a theory, a hypothesis, since I have lost the ability to scientifically prove their existence."

"What are Strings?" Mary asks.

"I believe they are the architects of all energy and matter in our universe. They vibrate at different frequencies, blinking in and out of 'existence'."

"Okay, I wanted to go back to the beginning with you anyways, Dieter, when you said that everything vibrates."

"Sure, let's start there." He pulls a string from his shirt pocket and ties a knot at one end. He then slips the knotted end into a cut in the wooden table pulling up on the string with his other hand. The string is now taut. Dieter begins to strum at the string, making it vibrate.

"You see how the more I flick the string the faster it vibrates?"

"Yes," Mary and I answer in unison.

"And do you see how it almost disappears from view, the faster it goes?"

"It's funny, I hear it too." I stare blankly at the buzzing string as Dieter continues to flick it.

"Everything vibrates like this on a quantum level. We are made up of vibrations, and so is this table, and this string." Dieter grins and closes his eyes. "Like music, yeah?"

I see a 'eureka' moment play out on Mary's face.

"I listen to music when I'm having difficulty with my meditation," she admits. "I *feel* the music and it helps to center my thoughts."

"Exactly!" Dieter's hand pounds on the table." You *feel it* because music *is* vibration and it touches you on a level that transcends the physical world. It interacts with those quantum vibrations that live within us all!"

"What does that mean exactly?" I ask.

"It goes to my point that we can be affected on the quantum level. If music helps send Mary into that plane of meditation where she may walk with *God* in the quantum dimensions, then my work is being realized as we speak!"

"Because…"

"Because you *feel* music." His fingers point frantically at his ears. "You hear sounds. Sound is not a tangible thing, but a wave of energy, you *feel it*. And that it is the vibrations from the music which helps send Mary into a meditative state, those vibrations are affecting her own frequency propelling her spirit, into the quantum level!"

"Perhaps you should learn to play an instrument," he suggests.

"I would like to learn to play the piano, but I'm told it is out of tune,"

"You have a piano here?" Dieter perks up.

"In a room off the library, but it needs tuning and no one here knows how." Mary's face drops.

"I know how." Dieter urges us to move. "Please, show me this piano and I will fix it for us."

Mary and I rush out after an almost delirious Dieter, anxious to hear the ancient instrument brought back to life. Mom had spoken of my grandparent's piano, and how it used to soothe her to sleep as a child. A gift of music was always welcome, and if Dieter could really tune the piano, it would be a great gift for the entire community.

Chapter Sixteen

Mary, I am certain, has found herself here by way of destiny, not only for her, but for me as well. I sense during every moment with her that epiphanal feeling that it is 'meant to be'. These stirrings have alerted me to what I have been missing: love, on a physical plane. Not the love of a friend. Not the love of a mother, though no one could replace her for me. This is altogether different. I feel it in a very physical way. There is a tingling in my chest when I think of her. Electricity excites the hairs on my arm when we touch. I smile without thinking, feel a sense of independence in her presence and a freedom I have only known in deepest meditation.

In the mess hall, mom is resting her head in her hands, grinning from ear to ear as I tell her what's been happening to me during the past couple of weeks with respect to Mary.

"Yup!" she exclaims. "That's love." Her hands reach out for mine. "I've been wondering when it would happen."

"Well, then, what do I do about it?" I ask finding it hard to catch my breath.

Mom's face turns suddenly serious. "Do you know if she feels the same?" I know mom was once in love with the Sergeant. She called it unrequited love. A sad story, and it shows now in her face.

"I think so. But, how can I be sure?"

She squeezes my hand. "Leif, you just ask her then. There is no joy in not knowing. There is less joy than in knowing she doesn't, but then you can get over it, or work on it. But ask her."

"How do you ask someone that, Mom?"

"Tell her how you feel." She's squeezing harder now. I let her nails dig into my palm without a word. "She will be more than happy to tell you if she's feeling the same."

"And if she isn't?" I can't say I'd thought about it much from that angle, but saying the words aloud took the tingling sensation from my chest and landed it firmly in the pit of my stomach.

"It's early still," she says, leaning back. "Maybe it's too soon to ask something like that." I must look confused. Was she changing her plan because she thought it unlikely Mary could have fallen for me as quickly?

"Maybe," I say looking down at my hands.

"You do what you think you should do, Leif. Don't listen to your silly mother." She's smiling again as I look up at her. "Young people fall in love quickly like that. I remember." Now she is looking at her hands.

"I'll know what to do the next time I see her. I'll just know." I wish my feelings were as sure as my words.

Chapter Seventeen

The sanctuary is well hidden by Castle Peak, the towering three hundred foot-high mass of jagged rock jutting up just a few yards north of the base, creating a sheer cliff along the south-west expanse of the lake. Elle Lake itself, which cuts around the trees and gardens in a long semi-circle until it comes to the hills rising up in the east, offers only a southern passage and potential eastern approach, both of which are heavily guarded.

It is ideal. The fishery is directly off-shore and there is netting laid a hundred yards in every direction to fence in the fish, preventing them from disappearing into the areas untouched by the zebra mussels, which were employed to clean the lake floor of the fall-out.

Elle Lake is where the Chaplain's efforts to rebuild our world are really beginning to shine. His work in populating the indigenous fish that once teemed through the waters and planting such a variety of vegetation, the majority of which once thrived here, have paid off.

The blossoms bloom in the summer sun and their perfume is exhilarating. It is a crime to pick a bloom, as these will one day be edible fruit, and I fight off the urge to hand one to Mary.

The day is warm and the sky a brilliant blue. The lake carries with it a breeze that catches Mary's new growth of hair.

She has gained a little much-needed weight since her arrival and looks even more beautiful than when I first laid eyes on her. Even her lips have grown fuller and her skin more radiant. I love to hear her laugh and as the wind picks up she laughs louder.

I take Mary to my sacred hollow that sits in the center of a small pine forest.

"This is gorgeous, Leif." She spins around.

"Sit with me a moment, Mary." I pat the soft forest floor in front of me. Mary sits and, closing her eyes, takes a deep breath.

"This is more fragrant than the forest on the base."

"We have very few cedars and pines behind the walls. The Chaplain says they do better out here, close to the water."

"Can we drink the water?"

"Not directly. Not yet anyway."

"But it works for the trees." She touches a white pine's rough trunk and smiles.

"Yes, the soil from our compost is rich in minerals and helps to filter the water so the tree isn't poisoned. We get our drinking water from underground wells."

"What's your favorite fruit?" she asks playfully.

"I don't have a favorite fruit."

She smiles and leans in to kiss me.

I meet her lips. My heart is racing. Can she hear the thumping in my chest? Mary puts her hands on my knees. I feel her touch throughout my entire body. I hope for the moment to never end. Just as this thought occurs to me, Mary pulls back. She looks at me intensely for a moment. Then, as if almost frightened, she speaks.

"I'm happy, Leif," she says. "I'm so happy with you." A shy smile appears and her face reddens.

I'm so sure I love her. I feel as light as air, yet the trepidation I feel in my stomach when I think to tell her… it's all very confusing.

"Leif, do you think we were meant to meet? I mean, you believe things happen for a reason, right?"

"Yes. I always have." I hope she's going where I think she's going with this line of questioning.

"I think I believe that too. I think if we weren't meant to meet and be a part of each other's lives we wouldn't have."

I nod in agreement, though my enthusiasm is underwhelming. Not because I disagree in any way, but because I feel myself leaving my body.

"Don't you?" She looks at me, tilting her head.

"I do," I reply. And with that the impulse strikes me.

"I love you." I feel the heat in my cheeks burn to the surface. A beacon of my humiliation; I think. What's wrong with me? Mary straightens and there is a pause as she looks me in the eye. I've made a very pleasant moment tense for her, I think. She doesn't feel the same way. This is all falling apart. I'm an idiot. Just when I feel I can't possibly last another moment without another word being uttered, she springs forward, wrapping her arms around my shoulders and forcing me back into the spongy soil. She then proceeds to kiss me in short explosive pecks all over my face and head and neck. I giggle as her tickling breath accompanies each kiss and am overjoyed at her response to my declaration.

We roll around among the pine needles and I kiss her passionately; our tongues rolling over one another's. Then she slides on top of me and pins me to the ground.

"I love you, too," she says very slowly, her lips swollen and pink.

Her shifting weight on my pelvis excites me and I pull her down to my left to avoid any further embarrassing affirmations. My vision is blurry and my words now stick in my throat. I can smile, but that's about all I can do. She leans in to kiss me again and the urge to fall into her, recklessly, and without thought of our surroundings, ignites a fire inside me.

Mary pulls away from me. "Do you want to?" she asks in a whisper.

I know what she's asking, and yes, oh *god* yes, I *do* want to. I nod like an imbecile. She stands up and offers me her hand. I grab it. We rush through the sanctuary, past the guards, the vegetable gardens, the brick oven, row upon row of apple and pear trees, the blueberry bushes, every new obstacle seemingly placed to make our escape more difficult. Running the perimeter of the base we rush through the gates and push through the residence doors, Mary leading the charge.

When we arrive at her room she fumbles with her keys. Once the key turns in the lock Mary shoulders the door open and drags me inside. The door slams shut, the key still in the lock. Mary hurries off her outer layers of clothing and I stand there watching her reveal herself to me, dumbfounded. Mary slows and then stops.

"What are you waiting for?" She grins at me. I snap out of my stupor and burst three buttons on my shirt, tearing it off. My pants fall away and we're on Mary's bed kissing and pushing our bodies against one another. Her flesh is hot. I feel like I have a fever and the only way to quench it is to satisfy this intensifying urge to bury myself in Mary. Her under-things are now on the floor and she's pulling at mine. I let her. We're both trembling. The thrill of connecting like this with another person is unlike anything I had imagined.

I am present. I am Mary and she is me. We are one.

Chapter Eighteen

I've always known love. My mother's love, the love I feel when enraptured in meditation, the love of my community. Though these affect me on a physical and spiritual level, there is something infinitely more substantial about the love I feel when I look at Mary. I feel out of control. It's exciting and new and addictive. I love being in love with her, and it makes me feel amazing that someone so incredible feels the same about me. I have found my bliss in Mary. She is my soul mate, and I tell her this every opportunity I have. I do not want to be away from her, and when I am my focus is on when I will see her again. I see her face when I meditate and feel her arms around me. The physical aspect of love is far greater than I had imagined. When we are intimate in that sense I am present, in the moment, enjoying her and enjoying the life of a physical 'now'. I had never imagined the 'now' in the physical world being so perfect.

"Mind your feelings, Leif," Blank Man whispers to me. "You're drifting dangerously out of sight."

"What's that supposed to mean?"

"Your destiny, Leif. Your dedication has been misplaced as of late."

"Have I not done all you've asked of me?" Irritation rises in my voice.

"You have."

"Then let me have this. What harm can come from this?"

"Do not ask the questions if you do not want to hear the answers, Leif."

"Fine, don't answer then." Blank Man simply wants my undivided attention. After everything I'd done for him, living my life the way he'd wished, didn't I deserve a little happiness of my own? And wasn't the point of all of this to rebuild the human race? If I couldn't fall in love and have a family, what is the point?

"You still haven't *seen*, Leif. Your father's destiny is yours now and you must see it through."

"What do you want from me now?"

"You require more time spent in meditation and less in other activities before you can learn this."

"Just answer the question, please." I am becoming angry.

"You will learn your true destiny in meditation."

"I meditate five times a day!" My hands turn into fists. I was happy in every aspect of my life, but now Blank Man is trying to disrupt that.

"Why!? Why can't I have this? Why can't we be happy together?" I am thankful Mary isn't in the room to witness this outburst.

Blank Man leans toward me from the mirror. His head cocks and I throw a fist into his silhouette, breaking the mirror and cutting my knuckles.

Chapter Nineteen

I am angry with Blank Man and send him away each time he calls on me. I do not understand his disapproval of my newfound relationship. Am I nothing more than a workhorse to him? Plowing out his plans to the crack of his whip? Am I to have no life but that of servitude? When was *I* given a choice? I've been prepared by the Blank Man for some great purpose he won't reveal to me, yet I'm supposed to just accept it?

This night I sleep poorly. My 'Angel' constantly tries to push through the boundaries of my mind, to discuss this disagreement between us, but I force him out – for now, my thoughts will be my own.

*****

I do not sleep through the night. A new nightmare finds me. They are becoming more and more frequent. There is an urgency in this recent manifestation. A darkness approaches.

Chapter Twenty

The next morning at the greenhouse I find the Chaplain tending a new crop of indigenous fish. To our left there must be a hundred saplings - pine, fruit trees, deciduous. These will further fill out the forest by the lake in years to come.

"Good morning, Leif."

"Hello, Father."

"I hope you've come with conversation this morning."

"I have, actually," I say, as though that were something atypical. My arm rests against the plastic pond as I watch the tiny fish dart through the water.

"Wonderful." He picks up a mug of coffee from the pond's plastic ledge. He never starts the day without a coffee. Luckily, the base had enough freeze-dried coffee in its underground storage facilities to caffeinate one thousand soldiers for five years. The absence of those soldiers left enough coffee to serve the one hundred or so this base has housed at any one time for at least fifty years.

I enjoy watching the Chaplain sip at his cup. The look on his face as he holds the bitter liquid in his mouth and swallows always makes me laugh. He grimaces as I smile at him; this one vice he should be allowed to savor.

"You were a botanist before you became a religious man." I open the conversation with a statement we both know to be true. I am nervous about my line of thought.

He nods and I continue.

"And I assume you never married?"

"No, never truly." He closes his eyes, allowing the coffee's aroma to permeate his senses. "I did have several relationships with women though."

"Was it easy to give that up? I mean, have you ever been in love?" I look down at my hands so he cannot see how much his answer matters to me.

"When the spirit of the Lord entered me, all others became secondary. It was a calling."

"But you knew what love was before you were called?"

"I did. I was with someone for eight years when I was called."

"And were you in love with this person?"

"I was. I mean, I had fallen in love with her and we lived together for five years as I worked as a botanist." He pauses. "Was I still in love with her eight years later? I'm not sure. Love is a powerful emotion at the onset, but it fades over time. Being called upon by God to serve is not a love that diminishes, and for me it was an easy transformation."

"So you gave up the love of a woman to love *God* and serve *Him*." This was a difficult pill to swallow, if the Chaplain could give himself completely to his religion, should I not also feel this connection to the purpose laid out for me by Blank Man? But Mary… My heart skips a beat at the thought of her. I love her.

"Father…"

Before I finish my thought an explosion bursts in my ears, the glass wall beside us shattering into thousands of pieces.

Chapter Twenty-one

I waken to the sight of mom hovering over me. I am lying in one of the hospital bunks. When she sees my eyes open, she springs to my side and strokes my forehead.

"Thank God," she says.

I sit up and see that my right arm is bandaged from wrist to shoulder, and a wrap covers my chest. "What happened, Mom?"

"The terrorists are at it again." Her face is a maze of lines. I feel an urge to trace them with my fingers.

"*Earl?*" His name is still with me after all these years. Earl, mom's enemy and leader of a group of terrorists that has tested our bases defenses time and again. But, that was many years ago.

"No," Mom answers. Her brow pulls downward. "He wasn't among the dead, and those left alive didn't seem to know who the Sergeant was talking about before they were hanged."

"But you're alright?" She runs her hand delicately over my bandages.

"I am, Mom." I grasp her moist palm with my right hand and flinch at the many tiny sharp pains that travel up and down my arm.

"Oh, Leif, don't move your arm."

"Yeah, bad idea," I agree. I look at her again and see a sadness that goes beyond my superficial wounds. "Is there something else?"

"Oh, Leif." Her head bows and eyes close, and she stays that way for a time.

"What, Mom? What is it?" My heartbeat speeds up and my stomach drops.

Something was very wrong.

Her head turns to her left, and I follow her gaze. In a bed three cots from me is Mary. She is still, lying under a grey sheet with her head bandaged and a brace around her neck. I instantly attempt to go to her, but find the pain of moving too great.

"What happened?"

"They found her lying behind the northwest watch tower. She had fallen." Her hand moves to her mouth. It is a twenty foot drop from the crow's nest to the ground.

"Is she unconscious?"

"It's more than that, Leif." I feel her hand softly rest on my shoulder. "She was gone for nearly three minutes."

I swing around and stand. "Gone? *Dead?*"

"It was all we could do to bring her back, Leif."

"Is she…" I couldn't finish the sentence.

"We don't know that."

Tears escape down my cheeks and she wipes them away.

Putting on a brave face I say, "She will."

I am able to travel the short distance to Mary's bedside without too much discomfort. I sit, reading a book of meditations aloud. I feel at odds with my own theories and truths. That my destiny would steal away the woman I love makes me question everything. I am finding it difficult to fight away feelings of anger and discouragement. I should be happy for her, should she cross to the other side. But was she ready? I have so much more to teach her. I want her to be prepared for this end. And I, perhaps selfishly, want her with me longer. The love I feel for her is so different from all others, and that we love each other, total strangers, is incredible.

My leg involuntarily bounces on the ball of my foot. I continue to fight back the negative thoughts causing the unwelcome emotional responses.

"Leif," a small voice whispers. My heart leaps.

"Mary," I say, bending to face her. I leave the book and take her hand in mine. "Mary."

"Leif," she says again in a weak whisper. "Leif, I saw."

"You fell, love. You fell and hit your head. But you're fine, you'll be fine."

"Yes, everything will be fine," she assures me, nodding in spite of the neck brace. There is such a peaceful look on her face that I am unprepared for what happens next. Mary suddenly begins to blink wildly. Her eyes roll up into the back of her head.

I stand, not relinquishing my grasp on her hand. "Doctor!" I shout. "Nurse!"

A nurse rushes to my side and sees that Mary is awake and in distress. "I'll get Dr. Bren," she says, rushing out the door.

I sit again and gently kiss Mary's face. "Stay with me, Mary." Her eyelids cease their flickering and she stares at me.

"I saw, Leif. I felt it. It's beautiful."

Dr. Bren rushes in. He immediately takes Mary's blood pressure, tests her reflexes and shines a small flashlight into her pupils.

"Leif, let us do our work here," he orders sternly and I realize I haven't let go of her hand. "I'll come get you when we're done. Go get a coffee in the mess hall or something."

I nod blankly and back off. I turn and walk with a slight limp out of the hospital building, blindly following the Doctor's orders.

Chapter Twenty-two

I wander aimlessly through the streets that line the base walls. My heart races. The first thing Mary did was explain to me that she had experienced something marvelous. What did Mary see? I ponder this for three laps of the base. The thought had instantly occurred to me, but I let it roam around in my head: Mary has been to the other side.

I double back through the center of the complex, reaching the library. I throw open the door and burn a straight line to Tina, who is positioned where she always is during open hours: at her desk, her frameless lenses reflecting what information she is typing into her monitor. Tina's head pops up over her screen. "Leif!" she says, alarmed at my obvious distress.

"Where can I find anything on near death experiences?"

Tina gets out of her chair and rounds her desk to take my hand, and noticing the heavy bandage on my right arm, changes her plan and waves me forward.

"There are two hard-bound books here, but there are many more on the server, if you want to use the computer stations." She leads me to an open computer and begins typing the keywords into the base's intranet. A myriad of titles reveal themselves.

I watch her type frantically on the keyboard and study the screen as a dozen more titles appear.

"This is great, Tina." I scan each of the titles, deciding which to read first.

"Has something happened, Leif?"

"It's Mary, Tina," I say, "She's been to the other side."

"Dead?" A look of horror appears on her face.

"Yes, but back. She's come back!" I can barely contain my excitement.

"Thank God," she says, her hand falling on her heart. "Are you okay?"

I nod to my bandaged arm and shrug. "I'll live! But, I need to do this now. Can I stay here tonight?"

"Whatever you need, Leif. I'll be leaving in a couple of hours, but you stay on as long as you need to, honey."

I quickly flip through the two books Tina brings me and discover some very interesting information about the experiences others have had with this phenomenon. I need to know everything I can. Then I will be ready for this conversation with Mary. An inevitable conversation I'd always hoped I'd have.

Chapter Twenty-three

My duties as morale officer require me to visit with the friends and families of recently deceased members of our community. I have read up on the subject and trained myself on the approach. Though the Captain had no living relatives, and made no attempt to build a new relationship after her husband and children had died, the other three soldiers who had perished in the recent car bombing did have families who needed consoling.

After a few hours at the library I stand and stretch, resigning myself to the task of visiting with those distraught individuals, mourning the loss of their loved one. It's not something I relish, but I do feel as though I make a difference when I sit with them.

I step out into the warm summer night and watch a crowd of people rush past me. I stop Luke, a man of about forty, to ask what's going on.

He answers me excitedly. "Someone's lost their mind and climbed the big windmill!"

"Climbed it? Why?" We had several windmills on the property, but only one we called the 'big windmill'.

"That's what we're going to see." When I release his arm, he hurries off.

I naturally follow the crowd, my curiosity piqued. When I arrive at the scene I can make out a silhouette climbing off the last rung of the ladder and sitting atop the turbine. There is no breeze, thank goodness, so the blades are not turning.

"It's my brother," a woman tells the crowd. "He's sick: he told me he was going to kill himself." She's frantic. I watch as two men climb the ladder to the roof.

I shout up to them. "Don't rush up there."

"How else do you suppose we'll get him down?" One of the men shouts back from the roof top.

"If you charge after him like that he'll throw himself off. He's suicidal."

"There's no other way." Peter, the smaller man shouts back. "We're going up."

"What will you do once you're up there?"

"I dunno, grab him and drag him down."

"He'll never let you get that close."

I remember the woman, but I can't remember her brother's name. "What's your brother's name, Serena?"

"Marcello."

I move to the ladder, climb it and join the men on the roof.

"Peter, Jason," I address the men. "Marcello needs to be talked down, not forced." I thought if he was truly suicidal he'd have thrown himself off already. But if he's not, and is tested, he may jump anyways.

"Be my guest." The man steps off the ladder and on to the roof top.

Sergeant Jones appears on the roof a moment later with KC and two others.

"You're not going up there," the Sergeant tells me.

"Yes, I am."

"It's sixty feet up, if you fall."

"I won't fall," I insist. "Besides, who's better suited to do something like this?" I'd have volunteered the Chaplain, if her were thirty years younger, and it dawns on me that I haven't seen him since the explosion.

The Sergeant looks at KC and has to concede my point.

"But your arm, Leif." KC motions towards my bandage.

I bend my arm in the thick wrap to show how much movement I have. I bury the pain and smile through it.

"Give Leif your harness," the Sergeant orders one of the other two soldiers. "And here is the spare, for Marcello." He hands me both. I nod and KC helps me with mine.

"When you get up there, Leif, place this pulley assembly on a flat surface. It's magnetic and will act as your life line. We'll have the other end of the rope down here, understand?"

"I understand."

It takes only two minutes for me to climb to the top and once there I slow to a crawl.

"Marcello, it's Leif." I've seen Marcello at my classes once or twice with his sister. I had the feeling he had been coerced into attending.

"Oh, no, no, no, no, please don't do that. I'm not up here to talk to anyone."

"I just need to know you are okay, Marcello."

"I'm not."

"Why?" His nervous energy was beginning to get to me. I feel his angst and fight it off.

"You can't understand why."

"I will listen though." I watch Marcello pace along the hood of the turbine, and gently place the magnetic pulley system on the steel casing.

"That would be a first," he says, his hands balled into fists as he moves from one end of the turbine to the other. "No one listens to me, not my sister, not the people in the kitchen I work with, no one."

"Could I sit with you up here and listen?"

"What difference would that make?"

"Okay, then it's alright if I come up?"

"Doesn't make a difference," he assures me. So I climb the last rung in the ladder and sit on the high perch. It doesn't look this big from the ground, but it's actually very spacious: ten feet long and five feet wide.

"You're making me nervous pacing like that, Marcello. Would you sit with me?"

"I'm not doing this to upset anyone."

"Then why are you up here?"

"To jump."

"And you don't think that would be upsetting to anyone?"

"Who would miss me? I'm invisible."

"I see you fine, Marcello."

"Okay, I'm not invisible, but I might as well be. No one listens to me. No one lets me do anything. I'm useless here."

"No one here is useless, everyone's role is important to the community."

"I can't go back there now, look at them all watching me. I might as well jump and save myself the humiliation."

"Your sister is down there. Do you want her to see you hit the ground? Would you like her to live with the image of her brother, who she loves, slamming into the earth?"

"Goddamn it." He falls to a seated position and rocks back and forth, his fingers pulling at his hair. "I can't even do this right!"

"That's not a bad thing."

Surprisingly, a giggle escapes his lips.

I laugh as well hoping to encourage more laughter from him. It works. I crawl over to him and sit once more.

"Do me a favor would you, Marcello?"

He looks at me, quizzically. "Do you a favor?"

"Yeah, a small favor."

"What?"

"Talk to me. I'm a little nervous up here."

He nods.

"I'm not up here to tell you how to live your life, but you should understand the consequences of your actions."

"Consequences?" He begins to pace once more.

"Yes, well, your sister for one."

He steadies himself and breathes in deeply. A shudder can be heard through his throat and chest as he exhales.

"I didn't want to hurt her."

"But you know you will if you jump."

"I wasn't thinking of anyone else."

"That's the trouble when people act out of selfishness."

"I'm not like that."

"I know that, that's why this is so hard for you."

"I just can't exist like this anymore. No one listens to me."

"Well, you've got my attention, Marcello, I'm listening!" A smile pulls up the corners of my mouth.

"I feel useless!"

"You're not. You have to believe that. Look at all the people that have come to your side. They want to help. They're worried for you."

"They're here for a show." His eyes widen as he stares down at the crowd. "Why now? Why care now?"

"Because we're all in this together, and when one of us is hurting, we're all hurting." His nervous energy is spiking. He gets up and makes two more passes on the turbine and I am honestly getting a bit scared of how this is going to end.

"They pick on me."

"They pick on me too, Marcello." I pause. "But how you deal with it makes all the difference. This isn't dealing with it. This is running from it."

"I guess."

"You know that's what you're doing."

"It's so hard."

"It doesn't have to be." I motion to him. He flinches and moves further from me.

"Come down with me," I show him the harness. "Hug your sister."

"I'm sorry." He tells me, shaking his head.

"You don't have anything to be sorry for. We all have weak moments."

"No, I'm sorry, Leif."

I have little time to react as he bolts for the edge of the turbine. I grab at his ankle and his heal connects with my chin. My grip fails. In a last ditch effort I lunge at him with my wounded arm and manage to pull him down. Sergeant Jones and KC join me and secure the other harness to Marcello.

I am upset it went this way and sit on the turbine to ruminate over my approach. Tiny spots of red pepper the bandage on my right arm. I've reopened some of my stitches.

As the Sergeant hauls a struggling Marcello over the edge, KC manning the rope, I watch them land to cheers and applause.

Chapter Twenty-four

After the attack on the base, we count our losses. The Captain and three soldiers were killed in the explosions. An explosive device was thrown into the cab of their jeep while on a routine sweep of our parameter. The force of the explosion pushed Mary off the watch tower and onto the forest floor.

The second explosive, which put me in the hospital, had sailed over the walls, exploding on impact with the greenhouse.

The Sergeant was having a harder time than he wanted to admit. All of this was wearing on him.

I watch as he approaches from the east. I am cross-legged, nursing my newly bandaged arm on the forest floor where Mary had fallen. He is dressed in full military regalia, armed to the teeth.

"Do you mind if I join you?"

I nod and motion for him to sit. I look at his red and swollen eyes.

"How are you coping?" I ask.

"Not well, Leif," he admits, wringing his hands.

"Can I help?"

Sergeant Jones stares at me a long while, long enough to make me feel uncomfortable. He sucks in a deep breath and exhales roughly.

"It has become very apparent to me these past few months that you are a leader, Leif. I say this with conviction. The people love you. They are connecting with your ideas. You are meant for something greater than this."

His hand shoots out in front of him, panning the landscape, the ruined greenhouse beside us.

"Well, not everyone is so accepting, but I appreciate your kind words, Sergeant."

"These are more than just words, Leif. This is a request. I'm asking you to share the load of leadership."

I stare at the Sergeant, dumbfounded. "Wouldn't that honor fall to you alone, now that the Captain is gone?" I respond tactfully.

"Yes, of course, I will take command of the soldiers and run the military aspects of the base but, I am not the politician the Captain was. It is because of her we enjoy the relative peace we do inside these walls. Leif, your mother has told me what you're capable of. She's told me you could change everything, and I believe her. The way you live your life is very attractive. You have *disciples* for Christ's sake." He stops himself and studies the ground.

"I'm impressed at how you handled the jumper last night. It was inspired. You have it in you to lead."

"I failed Marcello last night."

"You didn't, Leif. He's with his sister now, he's alive."

I appreciate the Sergeant's words, and I allow myself the peace they offer. Understanding the path my destiny is leading me down with his offer of leadership I tell him: yes.

The Sergeant's eyes blink wildly. A grateful smile lightens his mood. "Yes?"

"Yes, I will share the load." I watch as Blank Man hovers over the Sergeant, a blinding light pulsating from his now brilliant silhouette. My heart fills up with a heat that penetrates the visceral, teetering on the spiritual. My destiny has been realized, and is now in motion.

Chapter Twenty-five

In the hospital, I catch Dr. Bren moving through my peripheral. "Doctor," I whisper, rising slowly from the chair next to Mary's bed, my hand never leaving hers. "Could I speak with you?"

"Please."Doctor Bren motions for me to follow him.

"Back soon," I promise her, kissing her hand before resting it upon her chest. Mary nods and smiles weakly at me, blinking twice and then closing her eyes.

As we enter the doctor's office he waves for me to sit in one of the worn, plush leather seats. I remain standing.

"I would like to know the extent of Mary's injuries."

"Of course," he takes his seat. "Mary's reflexes and other motor controls are perfect, Leif. Her speech and memory and problem solving abilities are all excellent. She has recovered completely."

"That *is* good news."

"Yes." His eyes narrow. "But you knew all that, didn't you?"

"I figured."

"Then the question is not about her mental and physical recovery."

"I was hoping you might have some information to offer from past events. Have any other patients had a similar... experience?"

Dr. Bren moves behind his desk and opens a drawer. He carefully places a folder three inches thick on the desk's smooth metallic surface. "This has been something of a pet project of mine." He taps the folder with his palm.

"When you lose a patient on the table, you lose a part of yourself. Then you start looking for answers. First you look for the mistakes, you look at procedure and you wonder if you could have done something differently. Then, when all avenues have been exhausted, you look beyond the factual. You look for something more. Some point to it all."

"And this is your research?" I point to the blue folder laid out on his desk.

"Yes. I have had patients die on my table, but some of them came back. Like Mary." He sits and opens the file. "What those people said to me, about where they went, and what they saw and felt, has intrigued me." His long, narrow fingers trace the profiles of dozens of case studies on the subject of 'near death experiences'.

"Then you believe?"

He straightens up. "I'm a doctor, a surgeon. Though these accounts are inspiring, I'm a man of science. I believe in the visceral. If I can see it, touch it, if I can feel it, then it's real to me."

"But your file: you must believe on some level if you've carried this file with you all these years."

"No, Leif, I *don't*. These files challenge the statements from those people." He closes the folder and looks up at me. "Whatever it was your Mary experienced, it was not life after death. Not in my opinion. My research says her experience was that of an oxygen starved brain, calming the mind and preparing it for death."

"And how do you justify that explanation?"

"Through the research of great surgeons: those who've dedicated their time to the study and mapping of the human brain." He sits back in his chair. "I know what you believe, Leif. I respect your beliefs, and I believe in meditation, but I cannot tell you I believe in life after death. Consider what science knows. As the brain gets closer and closer to death it only fires in areas which are very basic to survival, closer to the brain stem: a fundamental and primitive part of the brain. So, when the visual cortex, the back part of the brain, or the superior colliculus, which is considered part of the brain stem are activated; *all you'll see is light*."

I sit forward in my chair, fascinated by his clinical explanation.

"And that point of light is surrounded by darkness. Our best interpretation would be of being in a tunnel. *Everyone* that has had a *'near death experience'* has shared this vision. It is much like dreaming, disjointed images, nonsense dialogue, it pulls from the same place. In near death, the central nervous system reanimates our most primal memories, our most deep-seated life experiences You could say your whole life passes before your eyes."

"So what about 'out of body' experiences. I mean, you're telling me the 'near death experience' is the brain putting a person at ease, but it is often accompanied by an 'out of body' experience. How can that be explained?"

"I can't explain that, Leif. I won't even try. I can only comment on the science, not on the spiritual."

"But you understand a man laying flat on an operating table, for all intents and purposes, dead, who can describe how many people were in the room and even what they looked like once revived isn't experiencing a hallucination."

"I'm not qualified to answer that, Leif."

"You are if you have an opinion, Doctor."

He laughs and shakes his head at me. "Sure, Leif, if I had to answer that I would say no, he's not having a hallucination, he's dead."

"What then?"

"Perhaps another look through my notes will produce a satisfactory answer, for both of us." He opens the folder once more.

"Thank you for your time, Doctor." I turn and open the door to leave.

"Leif," he calls after me, his tone pleasant. I turn. "Either way, she's back." A broad smile lightens his face. I smile back.

"She is, Doctor, thank you for that." I smile and return to Mary's bedside.

Chapter Twenty-six

The Sergeant and I walk toward the greenhouse, where Father Henderson and I were talking when the explosion happened. I take in the damage. The north side of the building has been shattered. The metal skeleton is bowed in the middle, all the windows gone. The vegetation and gardens inside seem unharmed save the thousands of pieces of plastic that litter the soil. Dozens of volunteers wade through the vast gardens picking out the plastic, careful not to disturb the plants, many of which are ready to bloom.

"It's a damn shame," the Sergeant says as he tosses a shard of window pane into the walkway where the volunteers are stacking it. "I'm sorry about the Chaplain."

I turn to meet him. "What?" I ask dumbly. "What about him?"

"Oh, Leif, didn't your mother tell you?"

"No."

He takes a moment to wipe away a pained expression. "I'm not sure I should be the one to then."

Anxiety rises in my chest and I realize I am holding my breath. I choke out a response. "Tell me, please."

"It's not my place." He explains.

"Sergeant," I take him by the arms. "What's happened to Father Henderson?"

"It's just, well, of the two of you, you were the lucky one." He squeezes my shoulder. I step back and shake my head. I hadn't felt so light headed before. The Sergeant's arm falls to his side as I move out of reach.

"What?" I manage. "Where?"

He approaches me with a look of concern. "I'm sorry, Leif, I should have let Sara - your mother - tell you."

I back into one of the raised ponds, my left arm sinking in the water. I let myself slide down to the concrete floor and sit. The Sergeant joins me.

"How?" I look at him. His head shakes slowly back and forth.

"They found him on top of you. He'd taken the brunt of the explosion."

"He saved my life." I whisper, my eyes darting from one crack in the concrete to another.

"Yes, you would have both been killed if he hadn't been standing where he was and you where you were."

"Can I see him?" My voice cracks with emotion.

"He's in the morgue."

We walk to the Hospital where the morgue is located in the basement. My legs feel as though they may give out under the weight of my building sadness as I stumble down the steep staircase. The Sergeant opens a steel metal drawer and there I see my mentor's earthly remains. His eyes are closed, his lips sealed tightly in an attempt to conceal his over-bite.

I hear the Sergeant move up the steps behind me, leaving me alone with my friend. I stand over him until my legs can no longer hold me up. I crouch down and steady my breathing.

Now I rest a hand on his arm and speak to him. I place a hand on his cheek, while a tear rolls down my own. "I'd never told you this, but I imagined you as my father." I am getting weepy now, but feel compelled to express how deeply our friendship touched me. I pull in a deep breath and continue.

"It has been a great honor to have known you in this life." I touch his chest and rest my forehead against the back of my hand. "And I will see you in the next."

*****

The funerals for our fallen take place over the course of one day. It is an opportunity for those that knew them to offer their remembrance, their love and their goodbyes. The funeral for Father Henderson came at the end of the day. Mom spoke eloquently for ten minutes; recalling her relationship with Father Henderson, and how her own conversations with him had given her great peace of mind. I carry out the Catholic rites as he would have wanted, and as he had asked of me some time ago should he die here.

Chapter Twenty-seven

The days after Mary's fall and her miraculous return to the physical plane were difficult. She slept most of the day and when coherent she would require assistance at meal time and during infrequent trips to the bathroom. Her family and I stayed by her bedside, as she recuperated.

*****

Terrible thoughts of Mary suddenly dying plague me. Though I should know better than to be sad for her should she suddenly pass, if she did die I would feel a great hole in my life, in myself.

So I decide to forego any meditation classes and all public appearances in favor of being by Mary's bedside. And when the doctor gives her the green light to come home, I roll her out of the hospital in a wheelchair, back to her room in the common housing sector.

"The doctor says you'll enjoy a full recovery," I tell her as we detour into the wooded corner of the base. "You'll be back to your old self in no time."

She reaches back and places a hand on mine. "Thank you for your love and support, Leif. I'm so grateful for you."

My heart soars as it does each time she professes her love for me. I want to hear that all the time now, and I am anxious to show her again how much I love her.

"And when can you take your bandages off?" She gingerly strokes my arm.

"Tomorrow," I tell her. "Mom's going to remove them and check the stitches. I have a lot more movement now than I did a week ago."

Tyrell greets us as we stroll slowly into the canopy of trees, escaping the heat of the day. "Hello, Mary." He bows to her and then looks back to me. "Will there be any classes this week?"

"No," I say with conviction. "All my focus is on Mary now."

Tyrell is stunned.

"When can we expect you back?" he stutters.

"Please let the others know I will return when Mary is well." Tyrell looks at us and bows again.

As we continue our walk in the woods several others approach Mary and I. They ask the same question Tyrell did. In order to deflect their concerns I decide to announce who will take my place until I return.

"Please, speak with Daniel," I say. "He can lead the meditation during my absence." Daniel is only sixteen, but a quick learner, taking to the concept and practice of meditation from a very early age.

"Daniel is so young," says Jessie, stepping forward. She is in her thirties, a survivor from the east, who joined us when I was only six.

Mary looks up at me and I can tell she is uncomfortable with the attention.

"Daniel!" I call as his slight frame moves through the crowd. He joins me. "Daniel will lead the classes until I return."

Daniel turns and looks up at me, confused. "Me?" He whispers.

"Yes, Daniel." I take him aside and lower my voice. "You will do fine. I need this time with Mary."

"Please hold meditation three times a day as I have. Repeat what you know." I place a hand on his shoulder and squeeze lightly. "You're ready."

Daniel is apprehensive at first, but nods at me.

"If that's what you want."

"That's what I would like." I explain.

"Okay, Leif." The anxiety leaves him and a genuine smile replaces the nervous one of a moment ago.

*****

"Will you tell me about your experience, Mary?" I ask softly as I put her to bed. The ambiance in the room offers an aura of calm, the corner lamp producing a supple yellow glow.

"I think you know what I saw, Leif," she says coyly, as she lays her head down on her pillow.

"I want to compare notes." I sit next to her. Taking her hand I lightly trace my fingernails over her forearm. She closes her eyes and I watch as her pupils move underneath the thin skin of her eyelids. Her mouth parts as she remembers.

"There was a light." I think back to Dr. Bren's soulless description of what the light meant in his case studies. "It was beautiful, but not just the light, the warmth. I felt like I was being embraced by love." She pauses.

"That's the sensation I get when in deep meditation. Cloaked in a light so perfectly white and warm that you just want to let go, and allow a breeze to take you with it."

"I wanted that," she says, her eyes still closed. "I had no intention of fighting it." Her eyes dart open.

Mary's free hand rises to my face and strokes my cheek. "Forgive me, Leif. I don't have the resolve you do. I could not imagine fighting that feeling. I am happy to see you again, and happy to be alive, but I would have let it take me..." She stops herself, turning her gaze to the grey brick wall.

"If the doctor and mom hadn't fought for your life and brought you back," I say, finishing her sentence. The warmth of her hand leaves my face.

"Yes," she smiles again, but this time there is no joy in it.

"I just, I would have liked to have had more time there, in the light." Mary pauses a moment. "I saw my dad. He reached out to me, you know? I really wanted to take his hand. I have very few memories of my father. Mom says he was overseas when the bombs fell. I didn't know I'd never see him again."

Now she weeps openly, abandoning all attempts at composure. I lean close and place an arm around her shoulders.

"I hated it when he went away. Sometimes for weeks. I told him I *hated* him when he went out the door for the last time." She takes a deep breath and wipes the tears from her face with her knuckles. Her chin turns upward, trembling, and she again cries into her hands.

"You were only five, Mary. Your dad knew that. He knew you didn't really hate him." I say, rubbing her back. The convulsions ease after another minute and she wipes her face with her shirt.

"I know that now. I was floating on a river for some reason." Her eyebrows thread together as the memory rushes back. "He was on the banks of the river. I called out to him, asking him to join me on the raft. But he shook his head. I screamed for him to come with me. He said he'd be waiting and disappeared from view."

"Be grateful you've been given this gift, it's a glimpse into your next life. It is a rare thing."

Mary smiles at me. "Your mother said I was the only one on the base who had ever done it."

"You see, my Mary, you *are special*." I smile.

"There's more, though," she says timidly. "As I fell out of that world and back into this one I saw your mother and Dr. Bren and a nurse working on my body." A chill visibly shoots through her at the memory.

"I can tell you what they were wearing, what they said, everything. The lights on the equipment blinking, the feeling in the room as they beat my chest with their fists…"

"It's incredible what you've experienced, Mary. But you're here, with me now."

"I love you, Leif." she says, her face deadly serious, and if it weren't for her piercing eyes I fear I might laugh. I quell the urge and lean in, kissing her. Mary in turn wraps her arms around me and pulls me into her. Pushing away the covers I lift the oversized night shirt above her waist. Again and again we make love, our hearts adoring, our bodies entwined.

Chapter Twenty-eight

As I wake next to Mary I find her propped up on one elbow, staring at me.

"I'm fine, you know Leif." She smiles and brushes a finger across my cheek. "You should be with the others now. Don't stay cooped up in this room with me. The doctor says *I* need to rest, not you."

I sit up and cross my legs, taking her hands in mine. "I *want* to be here, Mary. I want to look after you, be here for you."

"I know, and I appreciate your kindness, but I can't allow you to separate yourself from the others. Your work is important and you need to continue it. It's been two weeks. I'm feeling much better. *Much* better. You need to get back to what you do."

I am steadfast in my refusal.

"They will be fine. They have lots to meditate on, and you are my number one priority. You are *everything* to me."

"Listen to yourself, Leif." Her eyes narrow as she takes my face in her hands. "This isn't what you preach. You know better than anyone that this is an unhealthy connection for the mind. Don't center your attentions on me."

"Mary. I won't abandon you in your time of need." My head shakes as I speak, unable to comprehend her warnings.

"Leif, you have to leave me here and go to them."

"No," I say without thinking. I turn away, stand and make myself busy at the dresser rearranging the limited possessions she has brought with her.

"Please, I don't want to be responsible for you veering off your path."

"You have nothing to worry about," I say, still occupied with the trinkets. "I'm fine, everyone is fine. They understand why I'm here,"

"But do you?" she interrupts. I turn to meet her gaze.

"Of course I do,"

"When is the last time you spoke to your Blank Man?"

"I've blocked him out so I could be with you."

"Don't you see what you're doing, Leif? You've made *me* your *center*."

"So?" I shout, not meaning to raise my voice. Mary is caught off guard at my response. Frankly, so am I. I lower my tone. "I have given all of my life and myself to him and want only this time with you."

"To what end?" She rises from the bed and walks toward me. "Don't ignore your destiny for me. I'm no one."

"Don't say that!" I shout again. "Why would you say that? You're my *everything*, Mary. I *love* you. I never thought I could have this, but with you I can. Please, let me do this for you."

"That's just it. It's not for *me* that you're doing this. It's for *you*." She pauses to take a breath. "Can't you see that? Is your mind so clouded with love for me that you've lost your way?"

I turn and charge out of the bedroom into the common hall, anxious to get away from this conversation. She stops at the doorway and calls out.

"Leif, I love you, but don't lose sight of what's most important."

I stop a few feet down the hall.

"Please, *understand*, Mary, that *you* are most important to me." I feel a lump lodging itself in my throat and continue down the hall.

"Leif, we need to talk about this!" Her voice cracks and though part of me wants to turn back and embrace her I push through the outer door and into the grey day.

Chapter Twenty-nine

I'd spent the night at mom's after storming out on Mary. I complained that Mary was pushing me away when all I wanted to do was take care of her. This aroused emotions I had never felt. I *resented* her. It felt like the blood had turned acidic in my veins, my muscles hardening, filling up with the poison. A weight fell on my chest and I felt disconnected. Mom talked me through the alien emotion and settled my nerves, massaging the stiffening muscles in my neck. I fell asleep on her bed and awoke to see her sleeping on the couch which sat in a corner my childhood bed once occupied. Feeling a sense of peace seeing her sleeping there, I slipped quietly out of the room.

I return to face Mary. But now I am ready to face her accusations and uncertainties. I enter her room, which is dark and silent. Mary is not on the bed, where she should be. Instead, a note lies in her place.

Now, faced with this note, my muscles are set ablaze with the poison once more. I rub at my neck as I bend to retrieve the letter.

I've seen the light, Leif. I know your path is true. I cannot allow you to lose yourself in me when so many need you to find the light I have found.

Our time is over now. I see that. We have loved each other so much in such a short time. But we have loved blindly, recklessly.

Please understand why I am writing this and why I know I have to leave. My heart breaks for us, but I know I am doing the right thing, and I know you will see that in time.

You've shown me so much. I am eternally grateful. In this time of darkness you've opened my eyes, my heart, my mind. You are a blessing to everyone that meets you and I know you will do the right thing, as I know I am doing.

Don't let this act be in vain, my love. Go back to the people, for me, for yourself, for those that would follow you.

I am gone away.

I love you, always.

Mary

I realize I've fallen to my knees and am shaking. My sight blurs as the tears well up.

"This is it," I whisper through chattering teeth. The tears come in torrents now. My cheeks are soaked in moments. I drop the letter and it floats to the floor. My neck and back ache as they never have before. The tension building in my muscles is unbearable. My throat feels the size of a pin hole as I begin to convulse. I am weeping, howling now. Curling up on the floor by the side of our bed I wrap my arms around myself and draw my knees up to my chest. I want to run. Run out of the front gates and into the cruel wilderness after Mary. Chase her down and tell her she's wrong.

How has it come to this? What have I done? How will I survive this? I'm losing everyone. First Father Henderson, now Mary, who's next? Mom? The idea haunts me as I lay on the floor for hours, re-reading the letter, looking for something that offers a glimmer of hope that Mary would return. But I find no trace of such hope, and so I fall into hopelessness.

Chapter Thirty

The following days are bleak. I remain in my room, only occasionally opening my door after mom has knocked and left. She leaves food and water each time. I drink the water but find I have no appetite.

I read Mary's letter endlessly, aloud at times, hoping it will reveal some hidden meaning, something I've missed. I am ruined, I'm destroyed.

I question everything now. Did she ever love me, really? How could she leave me if she loved me? Were they just words? What's wrong with me that she would go to such lengths to separate us? The questions break me down, each one a little sharper than the last.

"Drama deconstructs love." Blank Man's voice sounds distant.

What has happened to me is unfair, I tell myself.

"This is self-indulgent," Blank Man retorts.

I am not speaking to him. My walls are down and so his words come through, but I refuse to acknowledge them.

I fear I am letting Mary down though. She asked me not to let her sacrifice be in vain. But what place was it of hers to sacrifice *our* happiness?

"She was right." Again Blank Man is in my head, defending Mary's rash solution.

Why couldn't I have both? Why couldn't I have everything?

"You know the answer."

In order to make sense of Blank Man's incessant input I would need to have a conversation with him. But I don't feel ready for that. In fact, I doubt the whole point to any of it now. Was I not to experience love in this life?

"That gift has been granted."

But it was taken from me.

"This too is a gift. You know the lesson. Meditate on your anger, your sadness, and your solitude."

Daniel is at the door now.

"Leif?" I hear his head rest against the metal door. "It's been four days, Leif." There is a pause. "Mary left another letter."

My heart jumps at this and my feet land on the tiled floor.

"It was to her parents."

This news is impossible to deal with right now. Her parents, her family, she's left them too.

"She told them why she left." Another pause, "Is it true?"

What could she have said? The fallout of this act would affect many more lives than just mine. But mine was all I could focus on now.

I listen as he pushes off, eventually. His footfalls travel down the hall, slowly, probably anticipating me throwing the door open and ushering him in. But I don't.

My thoughts turn from Mary's parents back to my own grief. My heart is broken. I'm in pieces. I was more when Mary was with me than I ever was alone. Her very presence was a gift. And that gift has been stolen from me.

"Mary's purpose was clear." Again the Blank Man disrupts my thought processes.

"Mary's *purpose*?" I finally react.

"Mary has served in the development of your destiny. It is now for you to understand to what end."

"Mary was sent to *teach* me something?" I chuckle ironically. "A lesson? I don't believe that." I pace the narrow space between the bed and the desk.

"Meditate on this, Leif. You will understand."

"Don't tell me Mary was nothing more than a lesson to learn. What was it all for? To learn about loss? To experience emotions no one should have to? What? WHAT!?" I scream. My hands fly to my head. I lock my fingers together and crouch on the ground. I rock there on the balls of my feet for a long moment, slam my hands down so hard on the tile floor that they instantly sting to life. The sudden pain sends me to my feet and I shake my hands out.

"Do not dishonor what Mary embodied," he tells me. "Meditate on her and know what she knew. See what you refused to see in her presence. Be the man you were meant to be."

Rage now builds in me. Rage is unlike anything I have felt before. It is unnerving, dangerous. I want to shout and scream and tell the Blank Man to go, to leave me and never come back, but then it hits me. The rage passes, my fists unclench and I sit, cross-legged and breathe deeply. I have to control this monster inside of me.

Blank Man appears in my mind's eye and shows me a meadow. It is beautiful, more so than even our gardens at Castle Peak. I see Mary there. She is radiant as the sun ignites her pale skin. A smile grows across my face.

"What is this?" I ask my angel.

"Does it calm you?"

"Yes," I answer.

"Mary's image calms you?"

"It does." My chest is no longer heaving, my face no longer hot.

"Good," he replies. "Use her to focus your thoughts and emotions. Now consider what she's taught you. Once you have grasped this lesson, share it with Daniel and the others. It is paramount to everyone's path."

Chapter Thirty-one

After another three days and nights meditating on Mary's image, her purpose, and my life's path, I open the door to Daniel and invite him in.

Mary was the embodiment of impermanence. She was my lesson, my teacher, but she was much more than that. Mary knew that I was becoming too involved in the physical world. She knew that she was the cause and so the effect of distancing myself from my one true path. I love her more now than ever knowing she could sacrifice her own happiness and mine in this life so that I would not fail in my destiny as my father had. That she could leave this place for the unknown hardships of the world beyond was truly heroic. But that she *knew* the hardships she was taking on by leaving, speaks even more of the courage she possessed.

"My biggest fear is that I have condemned Mary to the worst life imaginable simply by risking loving her," I tell Daniel. For all his youthful appearances, his is an old soul as well, and so we are drawn to one another.

"Don't say that, Leif." The soft tone of his voice comforts me. "She made her decision. You didn't ask her to leave."

"No, but if I'd known this end was promised her, I would never have made an attempt to meet her."

"What would have come of that? What could have been learned from that?" He stands and circles me. "Impermanence, it's the foundation of your teachings, the core lesson you've preached to all of us, and for some reason, you have been given an example in your own life to draw from."

"It has been a difficult lesson." I remain on the bed. "But as you say, it has reminded me of the importance of impermanence in this life. That nothing in the here and now is forever, that everything goes away, in the end."

"Everything," he repeats. "An idea, a thought, you, me…" Daniel stops himself.

"Yes, but Mary is so much more than a lesson," I stumble with my words. "She is the person I love."

"What will you do?"

I take a deep, cleansing breath. "I could have her followed. Send soldiers out to search for her." A tear escapes me. "They could bring her back, and I could stay away from her if I knew she was alright."

"You think so?" Daniel pulls up the desk chair next to me. I look up at him, smiling sadly.

"No," I answer.

"And so ends the lesson."

Chapter Thirty-two

Though I have accepted Mary's leaving, her parents insist they will never recover.

Seated in the hospital, where Mary's mother has suffered a stroke, and her step-father has spent the better part of the week, I beg their forgiveness.

"If I could take back the last few weeks and return Mary to you, I would." I tell them.

Mary's mother is lying on her back, unable, or unwilling, to move. The only sign of life is her sporadic breathing, and the trail of tears that shows no sign of slowing. She is an emotional wreck, and I feel one hundred percent to blame for her predicament. Though I thought I was doing them proud by looking after Mary, spending every waking hour at her side as she recovered, I became the catalyst for her decision to leave the base, her family and myself.

"Please, Leif," Sam, her step-father says through clenched teeth. "Please, just leave us. We've asked the Sergeant to send a team out to find her days ago."

This news excites me, but days ago? She's hiding from them. She doesn't want to found. "I want you to understand why she's done this. Why she left us."

"It was you, Leif. We all read the letter!" Sam was becoming animated now. "This place was filled with promise. It was the light at the end of a long and winding road. And now…" He pauses to catch his breath. "Now it has accomplished the one thing we worked all of these years to avoid."

"What was it all for anyway?"

I bow my head, knowing the answer may not give them any peace. It has given me peace and reaffirmed my purpose in this life, but is there a chance these deflated people will see purpose in their daughter's disappearance? I must try to make them see that there is.

"I would offer you a reason, if you would listen," I say quietly.

Mary's mother sits up.

"Tell me then."

Sam is startled by his wife's unexpected reaction. Mrs. Gardener waves him away. Her aura is dark.

"Mrs. Gardener," I begin with a heavy heart. "There is more to Mary's letter than you may know, and more to our story than you may believe."

"Then tell me why my baby is out there in this cruel wasteland. Tell me why she's left her family." Her voice is raspy, and it carries with it a terrible pain.

"You did this!" She shouts. "It was you!" A sharp finger points accusingly at me.

My heart falls into my stomach. I feel horrible. She's right, it is my fault.

"Please," I plead with her.

"You should leave, Leif." Sam tells me.

My mind races to find the words that will console them, but I only stutter out the same plea time and again.

"No," Mrs. Gardener says loud enough to be heard by everyone in the room. "No you go! Nothing you say will bring her back. Nothing you say will change what has happened!"

Tears rush down my cheeks as I stand and obey her wishes. Fighting the urge to plead with Mary's family again I remove myself from the hospital and push through the door, utterly defeated by the sorrow that fills the place.

*****

That evening I hide in my room once more. I weep over the devastating reaction from Mary's family. Why did the words not come? Where was my Blank Man?

It takes hours for me to calm down long enough to center myself and steady my mind. I am exhausted. I sit cross-legged on my bed and rest my palms on my knees. My back straightens and my head falls forward, eyes closed.

Suddenly I feel a tug on my spirit. I am being pulled out of my body. I allow the energy to guide me, and steer my consciousness. A feeling of foreboding overcomes me. It is reminiscent of my recent streak of nightmares. I've never experienced this sensation when in the rapture of meditation.

It's Earl.

Part 2
Chapter One
Earl Speaks...

My trip through the second floor window of a burning building nearly twenty years ago wasn't exactly graceful.

I remember awakening to the thick smell of burning wood and drywall, which replaced the delicate scent of the bud we'd smoked moments before. I stood up in a panic, slapped Freddy on the head, stirring him out of a drunken slumber, and scanned the room for Kevin.

"What?" Fred shouted, sitting upright on the couch, blinking madly.

"The house, it's on fire!" I gathered a few personal items and placed them in a backpack. He stood and stumbled into the coffee table. "Where's Kevin?"

"I don't know. Last time I saw him he was complaining about a smell and left the room." Fred waved away the smoke that was filling the room above the three car garage.

"Right." I remembered that. I walked to the open staircase that overlooked the car port. "Shit, there's no way we'll make it through that." The flames were climbing the stairs. I turned and coughed violently as the smoke caught me in the lungs.

Freddy was at the door to the second floor. As he grabbed at the handle he pulled back quickly, his face contorting. "Jesus Christ!" The door knob was red hot. He waved his hand, blowing on the bubbling flesh. "What the fuck! What are we going to do?"

I looked at the windows. It was easily a fourteen foot drop from any one of them. Freddy followed my gaze and shook his head.

"We'll break our legs."

I threw the backpack over my shoulders and approached him. "We could try the stairs." I said sarcastically.

"Fuck." Fred repeated. Suddenly an explosion from below hurled us both into the west wall, and Freddy went flying through one of the windows.

Now the fire was racing through the addition, lighting up everything it touched. I realized it was now or never and attempted the door that led into the second floor. Wrapping my shirt around my hand I approached the handle. Then another explosion burst in from outside, shaking the whole house and sending glass flying everywhere. Suddenly I felt the scorching pain of a burning curtain mixing with the flesh on one side of my face.

Screaming, I flung myself through the same window Freddy had been thrown from. I landed hard on the earth below, narrowly missing the patio stones which lined the back of the garage. Looking ahead, I could see that the fuel tank had blown.

Pulling at the foreign material still burning its DNA into my own, I felt the skin of my face give way and screamed. I soon realized my mistake in crying out.

Gunshots coming from inside the house fired off sporadically. Knowing no one would shoot their way out of a burning house I realized that our ammo depot had been lit up by the heat.

"Freddy?" Cautious not to shout over the roaring flames in case this had been an attack from some unknown enemy, I crawled on all fours toward the back of the house. Looking up into the night sky, I watched as smoke billowed out of the windows, and realized that none of the house would be spared. I pressed the burnt portion of my face to the ground, rubbing some of the cool mud into the wound to stay the pain. Tears blurred my vision. Lying on my stomach I struggled to find Fred. Where had he gotten to in such a hurry? The pain in my face trumped the newly acquired shin splints, but I rubbed at them all the same, face back in the mud.

Then I saw them, two figures crouching behind the pool house. Squinting against the light of the inferno, I pulled my pistol from its holster. I began to crawl towards the pair.

The closer I got the more disturbing the vision. These weren't enemies per se, they were my house mates! The one darker than the other: Sidney! And the other one: Caroline! The whites of their eyes danced in the light of the flames. I watched them a moment and wondered whether they had just escaped the same fate I had. Then I saw they had two heavy bags with them, and water rations. They hadn't escaped at all! They had set the fire.

"*Sara.*" I decided to wait for her to appear before I shot them all dead. Baby or no baby, Sara had made a choice, and she would die for it.

*****

From the moment the first vote was cast, I knew I should have been the one to lead. Joel was unprepared. Shell shocked. A leader sure, but a leader for easier times. The Apocalypse wasn't exactly something every man was cut out to survive. It should have been me they voted for. Why Joel? The fact that we took shelter in his house was one of the deciding factors, I remember. What kind of quality was that in a leader? But we were just kids, and Joel was our mutual friend. Almost everyone knew Joel on a personal level. So it was decided. Joel would lead us. At least he recognized in me the ability prepare the defense of our stronghold.

When I consider the contributions I made, when Joel died, the house should have automatically passed the responsibility of leadership onto me. But they didn't, and the house divided. Why couldn't they see that it was *me* that gave our friends the level of comfort they enjoyed in the time after? When everything went to shit, *I* was the one who brought the artillery, *I* was the one who set up posts around the house and built the barricade, and watched the rain levels slowly drop. It was *me* who gave them hope!

I find myself dwelling in the past more and more these days, wondering how this end might have played out if I had been crowned leader instead of Joel. But that was all so very long ago. Eighteen years... nineteen maybe? Much has happened since then.

Sara, for example, *Sara* happened. Eight years after she'd lit the house with the intention of burning me and Kevin and Freddy alive, she walked back into my life. Running into her again eight years later blew my mind, and meeting her boy, Leif, Joel's son, was a trip. I saw them both in turn, from my cell in the base's stockade, where I was being held as a terrorist. First, Sara walked in to question me. *Where was my base, what were our numbers?* I was stunned at first to see her. I'd assumed she'd died with her unborn baby in the wilderness. But there she was, that superior look about her, holding her head high, smirking down at me. Christ, I'd like to have smashed that look off her face. I dream about it. I fantasize about killing her. My hands around her throat, squeezing and then, just when she's chasing the light, releasing, letting her regain consciousness and then squeezing again so she can feel death approach time and again. I can't help but smile at the thought, how I'll relish the moment.

Then surprise, surprise, her eight year old son walks into the stockade late one night, alone. He sits across from me; the iron bars all that's separating us. That was an interesting conversation. Although I did most of the talking, I still wonder what possessed him to go to the trouble of unlocking the door and sitting with me.

None the less, once the army had found my hideout, killed the men and brought the women and children back, my escape plan was in full swing. Sara thought she'd pulled the information from me, but I offered it under the guise of having let it slip. If I hadn't given up the location, my woman wouldn't have been brought into the base, thus locating and freeing me. We scrambled under the wall at a point in the base's defenses where the earth could be dug out enough that we could slip our thin frames under, undetected.

Now, after ten years in a strange land, just a few day's journey from the base - where I can say in no uncertain terms - my arch enemy - my nemesis resides, I have rebuilt my army, and it is many, and it is hungry.

Chapter Two
Leif

I have seen the beginning of the end of our time here. A great army writhing in desperation, anger and jealousy approaches from the west like a plague.

"Earl," I tell myself, waking from the nightmare. My sheets are drenched in sweat, my heart is pounding fiercely. We are soon to be overwhelmed by an evil with an appetite for destruction.

I must speak with the Sergeant. He needs to know what is coming.

Chapter Three
Earl

I want to meet Leif again. It's a strange feeling I have fostered since I escaped the base. Something compels me. Strange whispers in the night, his name repeated in my dreams. Why did he come to see me all those years ago? The questions have tormented me. I'm not losing my mind, I'm too strong for that. No, it's more than that. A destiny I have to fulfill.

We set out a month ago to return to the base. Perhaps they are all dead from another round of the plague? Perhaps they are stronger than ever. Either way, I've made it my mission to return. And I will meet them on neutral ground, with an army behind me.

Just days from my goal, the troops are restless with the promise of battle and the potential locked away in that place. Food and water await, and if I can't have it, then no one will.

*****

I see the skeletons of the past as I look upon the forest separating my army from the base. All seems still. Castle Peak towers over the plains to the north, and hidden behind it, Elle Lake. A hill climbs skyward just beyond the fortress' east wall. I approach from the west.

With twelve of my best men, I march through the woods, a white flag tied to two of my soldier's arms, our weapons hidden behind fallen trees a short distance behind us. Soon the base's west wall is barely twenty yards away.

"Stop!" A sharp voice calls from above and we obey. The pair of guards in the tower have their automatic weapons trained on us. "State your business."

"I am Earl," I shout back. "I've come to speak with Leif."

"Circle round to the south gates. You will need to be searched before entering the compound."

I watch as one picks up a communication device and speaks into it. He waves at us to move towards the gate. I nod to my men and we cautiously make our way round the tall steel walls I had tested time and again so many years ago.

At the front, between us and them is a repaired version of the gate my men had slammed through ten years earlier with one of the base's own trucks. It was a failed attempt to take the base, but a learning experience all the same.

There, looking out at us, is Sara. She, of course, is not alone, flanked by a dozen soldiers, weapons drawn.

"*I can't believe it.* Why would you return? Why shouldn't I gun you down right now?" she screams at me.

"Sara." I speak through clenched teeth, faking a smile. "Good to see you too." I bow, not taking my eyes off hers. She looks good: that dark hair, those big piercing eyes, and that body have not changed with the years. Jesus, she has kept herself up. I should like to ravage that body before I choke the life out of it.

"Enough with the bullshit, Earl, *why are you here?*"

"As I explained to your watch tower, I'm here to speak with Leif."

"Why would you need to speak with my son?" She is rattled at that. I am enjoying this.

"It does not concern you, Sara."

"Everything about my son concerns me." She pauses. "Shoot them."

I raise my arms. "Are you ready for war?"

Sara's hand rises from her side. "Wait," she orders. Her ability to lead these men impresses me. She has grown formidable over the years. "What do you mean, war?"

"What I mean," I say slowly, dropping my arms to my sides once more, "is if I do not return to my men within the hour, my army will attack this base with extreme prejudice, destroying as much and as many as they can with no thought for their own lives."

"You've rebuilt your army." Leif's voice rings out as the gathering crowd parts to let him through.

"Leif." My hands go out to him, my smile as sincere as I am capable, after what damage his mother's fire had done to my face. He is tall, like Joel was. In fact, it's a bit disarming that he looks so much like his father. But I know my enemy when I see him, and this kid is my enemy, whether he wants to believe it or not.

"We do not want a war with you, Earl. We want peace, but if war is all you offer, you will find no peace here." Even his mannerisms remind me of his father. The way he carries himself, the way his head tips sideways when he speaks.

"I must speak with you, Leif."

"So speak."

"No, not here, not like this," I approach the gate and shake its bars. "Could we meet on neutral ground?"

"We could. There is a patch of woods on the north side of the base, by the lake. Meet me there in two hours."

I point beyond the base, brows raised, and Leif nods confirmation.

"You remember Castle Peak," he says to me. "Just navigate around to the east side and follow the wall of rock to the lake. I will meet you there."

Sara grabs his arm and whispers something. I see Leif nod and whisper back.

"We'll see you there." I wave my men away from the gate.

As we march back into the woods I feel a warm glow on my face. I wonder if he will come alone. I will kill him if he does. But it is unlikely. The thought lingers though. Killing Leif, Sara's son, would devastate her. It would be better than killing her. She could live another forty years with the pain of knowing I took him from her.

We reach our weapons and gather them up.

"What's your plan?" asks Kent. He is nearly fifty and one of my earliest recruits.

"My plan is to meet Leif in his forest and *understand* him." I throw my rifle over my shoulder. "Know your enemy!" I say, kicking the dead earth. We change direction and march north. I send Kent back to the army to report on our progress, with the promise of victory.

Chapter Four
Leif

Seated on the forest floor, I watch as Earl and eleven others march into my sacred circle. Earl's aura burns like his dark red hair, but with a muddied green underlying the red. His slender frame looks ravaged by malnourishment as his ragged clothing sways around his torso, the scar on his face strangely appropriate.

My mother and seven armed soldiers form a semi circle behind me. Two more perch in the trees, guns trained on Earl's party.

"Welcome, Earl." I offer him a seat. He chooses to stand.

"This is some greeting." He is suddenly very aggressive, pointing at the soldiers. "And you claim to preach peace." His burn allows only a pained attempt at a smirk.

"I only offer guidance."

"And where does this 'guidance' come from? Is it the great beyond? Chasing spirits like your daddy?"

I ignore his contempt. "I'd like to offer you to a new path, a path of least resistance."

"Yeah, sure, offer *you* the least resistance so you can finish us off." He turns to his men and laughs, they respond in kind.

"In resistance there is pain, and suffering." I know Earl was nowhere near ready to respond to this message. All the same, I will only engage in a peaceful dialogue with him.

"You're as crazy as your father was." Spittle flies from his mouth as he speaks.

"Why would you deny yourself an opportunity to learn a greater purpose to this life?"

"This life is to live, to grow old and fat on the backs of others. Survival of the fittest, right? That's why we're here, to live *our best* lives." He turns again to his cronies for approval and they nod.

"And how is that working out for you?" I ask.

"My day will come." A bright lemon-yellow spikes in his aura.

"You have misled yourself and your group."

"I am what I am," he says, arms flailing. "The great I AM! That's what it is to be human: to exist, to excel, to know *yourself*."

"You distort everything to serve your own interests."

"So *enlighten* me." His arms stretch out beside him as his face pushes forward. His sarcasm is so thick; I feel it come at me in a wave.

"There is a new end approaching. You should listen, Earl, all of you." I address the men flanking him. "With this end, there is a new beginning on the horizon. You could be a part of that new beginning, or you could continue on your path, and be left behind."

"You're the one who's been misled, my friend. You're confused and you're confusing everyone around you. *This* life is all there is. Wake up!" He taps a palm against his temple.

His narrow vision of life is his greatest weakness. "If all you can see is what is in front of you, then you are lost."

"Fuck you, little man."

At this I stand, signaling the end of our conversation. My six feet two inches towers above his five foot ten. He backs up unconsciously, turns, and in a huff leaves the sacred circle with his eleven followers.

Mom calls after him. "What you do in this life will determine how you live in the next." He dismisses her words with a wave of his hand, not bothering to turn around.

I face mom and the soldiers.

"There is too much conviction in his words. Ego has overwhelmed him." I bow my head. There can be no doubt now, the end I have foreseen is the end we will meet.

Chapter Five
Leif

With the realization that Earl's army is here, now, I speak to the Sergeant concerning my vision.

"It's Earl," I tell him, seated on a tattered floral print chair in his family's quarters. "My vision saw a great army overthrow us, and I'm sure that Earl's men are the threat I've foreseen."

"This is it then? This is our last stand?" His eyes narrow.

"Yes, I feel certain of it."

He had trusted my ability to 'feel' the future for years now, and today was no exception. "We'll determine a defense strategy." His face is void of emotion, his voice stern and ridged.

"You're not understanding, Sergeant. I didn't just see an *attempt* to overthrow us, I saw it *happen*. We need an escape plan, not a defense plan."

"We can't flee our homes… it's too risky."

"We will all die then."

"A good death, one long overdue."

I'm stunned by his reaction.

"And your children? Is this a *good death* for them?"

He shifts uncomfortably in his chair. "What is there out there for them but a slow and painful death? A wasteland beyond our gates?"

I had never heard the Sergeant so negative, but understood we all have days where the future seems dim. Still, today was not the day to forfeit optimism. Today we needed a leader with hope.

"We have the lake; and the forest beyond our walls now. We could make a life there," I remind him.

"It's too close, if Earl's men take the base."

"They *will* take this base. That much I know for certain."

"If you're certain, I will consider this option." He stands and I with him. "If we run, then we take all we can. We leave them with nothing. Destroy the generators, the windmills, the solar panels, everything."

"A good plan," I agree.

"But, if they find no one, they will pursue us." I see scenarios working their way through his military mind. A smile flickers across his face a moment later, and he turns to me.

"We'll make a bomb."

Chapter Six
Leif

As the daylight fades, I walk the perimeter of the forest within our walls. It is an exercise I practice two or three times a day now. Here, I run into others on the base, all of us attracted to the life that inhabits the woods. Today especially, I contemplate a life beyond these walls. Dieter catches up with me.

He seems out of breath. "You know Leif, I just realized something and I'd like to share it with you."

"Please." I invite him to walk beside me.

"Whether your mother knows it or not, she is an anagrammatist." Dieter has that playful, whimsical look about him that always makes me smile.

I slow my pace. "That's a new word for me."

"Yes, and very cleverly done, actually, from what I know about you now."

"What is an anagrammatist, exactly?"

"Someone who can spell out a word or phrase and by rearranging the letters, pull another word or phrase from it. Sometimes this practice was used to pass on secrets."

"Why do you say that? Why is mom such a person?"

"Look at your purpose in this life, Leif. What are you here to accomplish?"

"To enlighten," I respond without hesitation.

"Yes, but it's more than that, and it is much simpler than that: you are to bring the people to grips with a life outside this one."

"Yes, to teach them what I know."

"Yes, but the message you bring is *life*." He stops and grabs my shoulders, looking me directly in the eye. "Your message is only this."

"That there is no death, save the transition from this life to that. Yes."

"Exactly, *Leif*." He winks then smiles at me, as though he were enlightening me to some great mystery. But as he speaks my name with a slow, deliberate, drawn-out pronunciation, I quickly rearrange the letters in my own name.

"*Life*," I say aloud. The veil of mystery Dieter had so expertly crafted lifts.

"Hah! Yes, Leif. *Life*!" He slaps me on the back.

A sense of purpose once again electrifies me.

*****

After dinner I find mom in the post-op. She is three years into her training as a surgeon under Dr. Bren, and as a result could be found day and night in the hospital, studying, or performing a simple procedure on a patient. She is in love with her new career path.

"Mom," I call out across the room. She looks up and smiles at me. I wave and walk toward her.

"Leif, what a nice surprise." She stands and we hug.

"I just had the most interesting conversation with Dieter." We sit at the desk and she clears away the books. "Do you know what an anagram is?"

"Is it a play on words?"

"Yes, at least, as I understand it, it can be. It's where one word or several can be broken apart and made to mean something completely different."

"Okay, sure, I know what you mean then. Tina has some games like that on the computers in the library."

"When you named me, why did you give me the name Leif?"

"Your grandfather's name was Leif. Why?"

"So you didn't pick it for its double meaning?"

"Well, I know it's Scandinavian, and that it means *loved*. Why the sudden interest in your name, honey?"

"Dieter pointed out that when you move the words around, as in an anagram, you get the word *life*."

She connects the dots right away and again places her hands on mine. "That's destiny at work for you."

"Isn't it amazing? How you can find purpose in something like a name?"

She nods again. "And just as you were doubting yourself."

"Yes." A lump forms in my throat. I had been so preoccupied with Mary leaving I had abandoned myself, and in doing so inadvertently abandoned my destiny. I stare at the desk, my head down.

"Leif, if Mary was meant to stay, she would have, you know that right?" Her hand wraps around my forearm.

I look up, nod and wipe away a tear. Though the logic is obvious in what mom says, I've held on to the feelings of loss and guilt. I keep them as a reminder of her, of Mary. Morbid, maybe, but I am having a difficult time letting go altogether.

Chapter Seven
Leif

I take Daniel up to the highest point of Castle Peak. An armed escort remains below us keeping a watchful eye. I have brought him here to practice a method of meditation I had not yet introduced to anyone.

Seated precariously on the rocky outstretch, I ask him to close his eyes and quiet his mind.

"Find the silence behind the noise. To embrace the silence you are embracing your creator. Experience the absence of sound. Hear only my voice now. Let my voice carry you forward. Let time dissolve and dimensions melt away. Find truth and *see*."

In our time on the mountain's crest, Daniel sees events unfold and an end so shocking he is thrown out of his meditation.

"It is our destiny to see this through, Daniel," I tell him. He is dazed and looks horrified. His head shakes slowly from side to side.

I nod at him. "Yes, Daniel. But remain hopeful, the best is still possible."

Chapter Eight
Leif

After my meeting with Earl and his group at the edge of Elle Lake, the Sergeant decided to double the guard. In the meantime, he carefully crafted a plan for the future. Unfortunately, my vision couldn't pinpoint an exact date, but the immanency of the attack had us both on edge.

Our men carried the most advanced weapons: fully automatic machine guns, grenades, even a rocket launcher. They were set up in crow's nests along the sides of Castle Peak's rugged cliffs and in bunkers that surrounded the man-made wonder.

*****

The Sergeant is a cautious man and skilled strategist, and whether he will admit it or not, quite clairvoyant at times. Just three nights passed before Earl's army attacked. The attack took place under the cover of night, the blackened sky making the gun bursts that much more dramatic.

The fighting was fierce, but short lived. Earl's men were quickly overcome, some killed, others captured.

The blasts woke the base, and many made it up the north towers, overlooking the bloody battle as it unfolded. I too watched as our soldiers gunned down the retreating group of twenty or more.

*****

The following day I get an idea. Having captured six men last night, an option I'd overlooked occurs to me. I pull the Sergeant out of the interrogation room, leaving the prisoners in the company of three armed soldiers.

"I want to speak to Earl's army."

"I'm not letting anyone from *his* group in this compound unless they're prisoners of war. None of them can be trusted."

"But there are children and women. I'm sure there are others that don't want to follow Earl, but do out of fear. Earl has manipulated them."

"Exactly, Leif, just like he had manipulated the girl who released him from our stockade all those years ago. Do you honestly think we could tell one apart from another?"

"I could."

"How?"

"If I concentrate on their auras, I can read intentions."

"You're a lie-detector now?"

"It's worked for me in the past. Please, Sergeant, you offered me a leadership role for a reason. I'm asking that you to get behind me on this."

His brow furrows. "And you can guarantee to me, *swear* to me, that you won't let a single person cross our gates unless you're fully confident they are done with Earl?"

"Yes."

"Because, Leif, as much as we're all very happy to have you lead us in our day-to-day, the protection of this base and its citizens still falls on me."

"Sergeant, I have every confidence in your abilities to defend us. Please, believe in mine."

He concedes. "Well, at the very least it may plant a seed of rebellion in his ranks. It can't do any harm to preach to them."

"Everyone should have their shot at salvation. These people are no less entitled."

"Can you see anything with these six?" He waves an open hand in the direction of the deflated and demoralized group behind the glass.

"I can tell you the two on the end want nothing to do with Earl. The others support their leader, but those two…" I point at the young men on the far end of the bench. "They are ready to leave him."

He nods, as if I'd just confirmed his own suspicions after hours of interrogation. "How do you want to approach the others? I'd suggest using the loud speakers, what with their squatting just beyond our walls."

"Perfect."

"This way you can get your point across without ever endangering yourself. When would you like to start?"

"Tonight, if you can arrange it."

"Let's speak to Salem about it."

*****

Salem, a forty year old man who maintains the electrical equipment on the base, sits up when he sees the Sergeant and I approach.

"Gentlemen," he greets us, sliding a palm across his shaven head and adjusting his glasses. "Is there something I can do for you?"

"There is, Salem."

"Does the intercom still work?" I ask. "I'd like to send a message over our walls."

"To the terrorists?" Salem is alarmed; his right hand unconsciously moves to the sidearm at his hip. "Why?"

The Sergeant interjects.

"Leif would like the opportunity to talk them down."

"Oh, stirring up some shit, eh?" He chuckles. His other hand moves to his chin, digging at the deep dimple. "I'm on it. Though we haven't used the loud speakers in a few months now, they ought to work." He scrambles back into his shop, where all dead electronics come to life again. He resurfaces with a component, holding it up for us to see. "I might need this," he says. Let's go."

We follow Salem through the parade grounds, passing the grave markers, and find ourselves in the control room. Salem slides under one of the panels and, cursing, slips back out.

"Something the matter?" Sergeant Jones asks.

"This thing might make a bit of noise is all." He flips a switch, picks up a headset, and blows into the mike. I notice someone walking past our window flinch and cover their ears. Salem then points for me to exit the building and confirm that I can hear him outside. I can.

Tonight I would offer salvation over suffering.

*****

Several speakers line the exterior walls of the base. A number of speakers also sit upon the rooftops of our buildings. I hear a low crackle of static in the air as I approach the control room.

Sergeant Jones stands at the door and opens it for me to pass through. He follows closely.

"We have doubled our guard in the towers should this cause a sudden uproar."

This news upsets me. My purpose is not to cause unrest, but to appeal to their sense of self.

"I'm not going to approach them in a threatening way."

"Just letting you in on what's what, Leif."

"Okay," I say and sit. I turn to the control panel. My arms go up as if to say what now? Salem assists me by placing the headphones over my ears and arranging the microphone.

"Just flick this switch whenever you're ready, Leif. You'll have no trouble being heard for literally miles just speaking at your normal level." He gives me a thumbs up and steps back, smiling.

I begin my appeal for the souls of those trapped in an impossible scenario, in purgatory.

Chapter Nine
Earl

The nerve of this kid. Who does he think he is? His words penetrate every inch of the woods. I run through the encampment, ordering everyone to cover their ears.

My generals do the same.

I'm panicking, I'll admit. This was not something I'd expected or prepared for. A fucking sermon! He was good, Leif. He understood the same basic principal of leadership as I did. Fear. I had them fearing for their lives and their family's lives, but this little prick was trumping me with an immortal soul. This would ruin everything. After our defeat at the lake, if even twenty percent of my army decided to leave, I don't think I could take the base. I expect roughly that percentage to die in the initial rush. I was foolish to have made that earlier attack. I hadn't expected them to be prepared, and my people were hungry, but regret now the impulsiveness of that decision.

And what if they do decide to leave me? I'd have to kill them myself. We'd have a rebellion in my own camp! What would the great leaders of the past have done?

I stand, my chest heaving as much from the running and shouting as from the anxiety of the moment. My head turns from side to side, watching my army listen to the propaganda.

"Cover your ears!" I shout again at one of the women and point my pistol at her and her child. They obey.

My generals surround me and shout the same order again and again, but I know I can't force this upon everyone. Many will obey, but many will listen to him. How I deal with it when it is over is what will make all the difference.

I listen now as Leif repeats everything he just said. Or has he recorded it and will now loop it again and again until it drives us mad?

"Should we shoot out the speakers?" asks Karl. He is the youngest of my generals, but every bit as ruthless as I need him to be.

"No," I answer, unblinking. "We can't let this rattle us." I wear my mask well. "They have the high ground and will decimate us. No, we won't be provoked into a fight. We wait until we are ready."

"When will that be?" I see the lust for blood pumping through his young veins.

I turn to him and slap him across his face. Karl staggers back, surprised, his hand shooting up to shield himself from another.

"Lower your hand," I order. He does, revealing a scarlet mark matching the back of my hand. I smirk.

"We attack when I say we attack. Not a moment before," I tell him, my voice rising over the loudspeaker, my finger now in his face. Karl lowers his head and turns from me. I look at my other generals. They have stopped shouting orders to watch the spectacle.

"Make it known they are not to listen to this propaganda!" I say, my voice steady and stern. All four walk off, repeating their orders to the masses. My attention returns to the base, whose west wall is just one hundred yards from our camp. Through the broken pillars of trees separating us I watch as the tower guards survey our reaction to this attack on the senses.

Chapter Ten
Leif

Sergeant Jones' son, Jasper bursts into the control room and reports his findings from Tower Two. "They're scrambling to regain control, Sergeant." Jasper is Jones' oldest, and a soldier at twenty two. The Sergeant has asked his son to address him as such while on duty, and Jasper doesn't seem to mind the formality.

"Thank you. It's working."

The recording Salem made is working perfectly. It is a brilliant idea, allowing the message to go on indefinitely. I have stated my position on this life, what they can all achieve if they walk my path, and explain the results of living the path they are on in the next life. I realize many of them have been too brainwashed by Earl for this to work on a large scale, but the few that may yet have the strength and presence of mind to leave him, will. They may do so at their own peril, but in dying for a decision as important as this, they will find peace.

Chapter Eleven
Earl

B y morning, the recording has stopped. Had it played all night? My dreams were haunted by Leif's voice. Had the damage been done? I stand, scanning the grim landscape, and hope that my army is still intact. My orders before I slept were to form firing lines along the east and south of our encampment; guns turned inward, firing upon any deserters. The equipment we'd been working on in secret was almost ready. My offensive on the base would be quick and deadly, and it would be soon.

Three women are brought to me.

"These three attempted to flee last night with four others: three men and a child," reports Curtis, my third-in-command.

"Where are the others?" I ask.

"They were shot."

"Dead?" I ask, stone-faced for clarity.

"Yes, dead," Curt answers.

"And why have these three survived?" I approach the women, who are being restrained by the other three generals.

"We don't throw women away so easily," Karl answers. "As per your orders."

I nod. "And which of these has produced a child in the past?"

"I – I have, Earl," answers one, the desperation in her response palpable. I eye her up.

"And where is your child now?"

"They took him from me."

"And you two, you don't have tongues? I don't remember cutting them out." I laugh sadistically and my generals join in. The women are frightened and visibly shaking.

Without hesitation I cut the throat of the one to my left. She gasps a last breath, eyes bulging, and I watch as her pupils turn upward, her body falling forward.

The other two are now trembling, crying for their miserable lives.

"Go back to your child," I tell the toothless one, waving for Karl to release her.

Turning to the remaining woman my eyes narrow. "This one we make a public spectacle of."

"No!" Her voice is cracked and dry. But she has no energy left to even kick up the dirt under her feet. She is dragged to a central point and tied to a tree. There she will remain until dead, her pleas for mercy killing the sense of rebellion Leif may have planted.

Chapter Twelve
Leif

It is my hope that many of those lured into Earl's camp through a basic need for survival, will take my words to heart, keep them close, and find the light in their darkest hour. I see their suffering from my vantage point in the tower, but hold onto the hope that I have done more good than harm.

*****

Daniel approaches me in the greenhouse to revisit the meditation we'd had on Castle Peak days before. It's time to convince him that his role is every bit as important as mine.

We talk under an apple tree. It gives me a sense of well-being to continue conversations here.

"Because we have seen what may come to pass, I need to know you are capable of carrying it out," I remind him.

His expression falls. "It isn't as easy as that, Leif."

I lay a hand on his shoulder. "You are my friend, Daniel, and I know what I'm asking of you will be difficult, but it is for the greater good. You understand that don't you?"

He nods reluctantly and looks up at me. "I understand." Tears fill his eyes and rush down his gaunt face, tracing the hard line of his cheek-bones.

I place my hand on his head now, a lump forming in my throat as I come to terms with my destiny. "You have doubts. You fear the unknown even after all that I have told you."

"No. I mean, yes." He looks guiltily at me.

"Do this for *me*, and you do this for *all* of us." I state taking his shoulders in my hands.

A look of determination suddenly plants itself on his face. "I would do anything for you. I just wish it wasn't this."

I release my grip on him. "But you will," I reassure him.

"Yes."

"Be clear in your mind that you must be prepared for this end, Daniel. If what we have seen is to occur, be ready, be strong." I am losing my composure. Turning my back on him I walk to the edge of the greenhouse. Turning once more, I smile at him.

"You can count on me." He nods, sucking in a deep breath. "I am that I am."

"You are that and more." I leave him, standing in the warm light of the greenhouse, as I march into a misting rain, and towards my destiny.

Chapter Thirteen
Leif

Mom sits, hunched over, on one of the cement benches that lines the north end of the hospital. Her blue surgical fatigues are coated in blood after assisting in yet another still-born birth. The rain has advanced from misting to spitting, but she does not budge.

"I'm so sorry, Mom," I tell her as I take a seat.

Mom just shakes her head. "That's six in a row, Leif," she tells me. Of course I know this, as does everyone on site. A pregnancy was rare enough the last few years, but a live birth was much more so.

"Do you know, Leif," mom continues, her head still down, hands crossed, forearms resting on her thighs, "the youngest person on the base now is three?"

I nod silently. The news is dire now. With no new births, everyone fears we will be the last. The doctor had predicted this long ago, and fed pregnant women what limited vitamins were left in the vast storage lockers underground, but they were proving not enough.

"Don't despair, Mom." I take her hand and she looks up at me, her tears mixing with the rain.

"Where do we go from here?" she asks, shaking her head. "If no more babies are born, what's left?"

I couldn't tell her what suspicions played out in my mind. Not now, not after what had just happened.

"All is as it should be, Mom. Trust in that." I offer a reassuring smile. Mom offers a sad attempt at a grin and pulls my head to hers. We bump foreheads lightly and I pull her up, walking her into the cafeteria, out of the driving rain.

Chapter Fourteen
Leif

I sit on my bed, preparing for my last meditation of the day, and find I am still thinking of Mary. Everything is for a reason, I tell myself. I lost her because I couldn't see what I was doing, I didn't *want* to see. I loved her so much I lost myself in her. I gave myself to her. I lost sight of my destiny and cloaked myself in her love.

I meditate on her image, I see her in my mind's eye as she was the day she left me. Sometimes I think I'm seeing her for real.

I wonder about her always. I feel responsible for her leaving. I have forgiven myself my ignorance and ego, but it is difficult not to wonder how she's coping in the world and want to go looking for her.

I find myself meditating on Mary exclusively today: her face, her hair, the color of her skin. I feel the heartache of her leaving, the anxiety over her safety, the depression over losing her. Strangely I feel I am losing control of my session: Mary's image is penetrating every corner of my mind. The sensations continue on a physical plane now as Mary's touch is remembered: the soft embrace of her lips, the scent of her skin. My head tilts back as Mary runs her fingers through my hair, her hands not stopping at my neck but tracing my spine and rounding my hips. Excitement builds to a climax as the vision melts into me and the sensation of being one with Mary overcomes my senses.

I open my eyes, lying on my back in my bed. Mary floats above me. She is dressed in a white, flowing gown, her face angelic. A smile works its way across my face as I reach up to touch her. But as I do, Mary drifts slowly away from me, landing silently on her feet on the floor beside my desk. She is smiling. I start to rise but she holds up a hand. I sit again.

"Mary," I say, my heart leaping out of my chest. But as I watch her flowing gown move in a non-existent breeze, I realize what's happening.

"Oh, Mary." The smile leaves my face and I fall on my knees, weak from the realization.

"All is as it should be," she says in a quiet echo. I feel the touch of warmth embrace my head, her weightless hand resting upon it.

"How did it happen?" I wonder through a tightening throat. "Did you suffer?"

"We all suffer, Leif," she answers cryptically.

"Please, I couldn't bear it if you suffered." I slide off my bed to my knees and my forehead falls to the tiled floor. I want so desperately to hold her in my arms, but know I cannot. Not yet.

"I am at peace, now." I look up from all fours and see her light barely contained by her apparition.

"You are beautiful."

"I had to see you again, my love."

A shiver rushes through me. I stop breathing.

"I love you," I say, speaking from my heart. Her light pulses. My eyes close and my head falls back once more. To be enveloped in her light is like a thousand gentle fingertips caressing every nerve ending.

"And I love you, Leif." Mary's light is fading fast, her features disappearing.

"No, please, don't go," I beg. "Talk to me, Mary, please!"

"My time is short here, Leif."

"Did you find your father?"

Mary's smile outshines the rest of her. "Yes."

"Good," I say. "What can you tell me of the other side?"

"Nothing." She shakes her head in slow motion, her hair moving as if submerged in water.

"Why?"

"It is not for the living to know."

144

"The Chaplain?" I ask. I must know.

"He is here."

"He knows now." I smile at the memory of his kind face.

"Yes, he knows."

Chapter Fifteen
Leif

Tonight I have a most disturbing dream. Horsemen charge toward me. A backdrop of blood red sky mixes with thunder clouds, spitting a thick, paralyzing rain from the west. A dark figure commands an ink black steed. I feel smaller the closer they get. Then they pass over me and I watch helplessly as the rider charges past.

I wake up with a start. My hands fly up in front of me, protecting my body from the pounding hoofs. I have never seen a horse outside of a movie, or picture book.

Did I see Earl's mangled face on the rider's head? I fear I did.

"They are coming," whispers Blank Man.

"Is that what that was?" I ask, swinging my legs out from under the sheets and hurrying out of bed.

"Your vision will be realized in hours."

"Hours!" I shout, looking about the room for my Angel. "Can I get everyone to safety in hours?"

"If you begin the process now."

I stand and rub my eyes. "What time is it?" I trip on my sheets as they wrap around my ankles.

"Damn it. Where are you?!" I ask, angry at his timing. "I could use your light!"

My guide appears at my desk and my room immediately ignites in a warm white light.

"Thank you!"

"You're welcome," he answers, his silhouette bowing slightly.

The clock reads 3:33am. I hear a pounding rain on the metal siding. It has been raining for days.

"He would attack us in this?"

"He will."

"Then let's get started." I get up off the floor, grab the head-set of my land line, and punch in the Sergeant's number.

"Yes," a faint voice answers on the other end.

"It's time," I say. I hear a click and my receiver goes silent.

The base has emergency procedures for several different scenarios. But this particular emergency has never been put into practice, until tonight. A level of calm must be observed in order to keep the retreat a secret. No lights blink or sirens sound. Instead, a group of ten will now be summoned to the control room and briefed on our next task. That task is to knock on each resident's door and escort them to the mess hall for a warning of what is about to transpire.

*****

Once everyone is assembled, I take the podium.

As I look into the crowd of survivors my heart goes out to them. Children cling to their parents, still half asleep. Some are restless. Others are angry, knowing what is coming, knowing they will be asked to either defend their home or leave it for an uncertain future.

What do I tell them?

"You've probably guessed why we're here, in the middle of the night," I start, my voice thundering over the fearful chatter of the congregation.

"The group of desperate people that have been living beyond our walls these past few weeks have decided that tomorrow they will begin an assault against us."

This stirs the crowd into more frightened noise.

"Please," I say, lifting my arms to invoke a sense of control. "Please, listen to me. We've prepared for this time. We know what to do. Please gather up your belongings, and meet back here in twenty minutes. From here we will head east: at the top of the hill we have dug out covered shelters into the earth. Remember, we must do this quietly."

Groans erupt from the audience. No one wants this. The Sergeant stands up next to me, taking the podium.

"Listen," he tells them. "I agree with Leif on the importance of placing everyone in our eastern bunker until this thing is won, but I want to call upon anyone that can and will take up arms in this fight to join me in the armory. I have sworn to protect this base, and I will do just that."

Cheers now ring out. I find mom in the crowd and watch as she spins, slowly, taking in her surroundings and those men and women cheering on the fight. I'd told mom what Blank Man had said to me. She knows that anyone that stays behind will die defending this base. She also knows about the bomb, and the plan should the Sergeant fail in his attempt to beat back Earl's forces. But any effort to talk anyone out of the fight would only deflate their morale, and I know many of the people here are ready to make the transformation.

I am at peace with the decision to allow it. Some were born for this end, as I am mine, and Daniel his, and mom hers.

I see fight in mom's eyes too, caught up in this whirlwind of emotion. She looks up at me, and we catch each other's gaze. She smiles sadly at me and I back at her. She nods and joins me at the podium.

"Let's get them ready to go," she says.

"Twenty minutes!" I shout and the group thins out, most of them rushing back to their rooms to collect what limited possessions they hold dear. They'll bring some food and water, though the bunkers have been outfitted with life's necessities for a few weeks.

Those who remain have committed to the fight. I see Salem. His enthusiasm over the defense of his home is inspiring. I also watch as Harry, Monty and Chris join the group. Harry frowns. He nods at me and I raise a hand. I watch as the Sergeant leads the men and women out of the mess hall toward the armory. Before he slips through the door he turns and motions for me to follow. I kiss Mom on the cheek.

"I'll be back to lead everyone out the front gates, Mom. I just have to help the Sergeant with something first."

*****

I follow Sergeant Jones and his company to the armory and notice that his wife is among the fighting few. Both her children have also joined the fight.

Once the group is outfitted, the Sergeant orders one of his sons to brief them on tactics until he returns.

We move through the halls to the kitchen, open the trapdoor to the basement, and descend. There, resting on a steel table is our bomb, and a simple counter set at one hour sits atop the monster.

"It will have enough force to disintegrate everything in this room, and the burst will take out the base right to its walls. No one will survive. If it's hopeless, Leif, I will set it after a few minutes. This watch will sync up with the timer on the bomb as soon as it self-activates the countdown." He straps the watch to my wrist. "This way you'll know how much time you have to *duck and cover*. I will light this flare if I determine that we have Earl's forces in retreat and then I will dismantle the bomb." He waves the flare in front of me. "If I succeed in shutting it down, your watch will tell you that too."

I study the architecture of the room briefly. It seems to vibrate around me. The energy waiting to be released is overwhelming.

The Sergeant slips the flare into one of the many pockets that line the legs of his battle fatigues. "We'll start pulling the components out of the generators and motors now. We'll meet you in the mess hall so you can take the bags with you. If we win this thing, it won't be any problem replacing the parts. If we don't, and the bomb doesn't work, and your plan B fails, at least Earl will never be able to produce a single kilowatt of energy."

I nod and move toward the door, hopeful this fight would not depend on my plan B. The Sergeant grabs my arm and gently pulls me to face him.

"We *can* win this thing, Leif," he says, looking for some affirmation from me.

I take his hand and squeeze it between my own. "Good luck, Sergeant."

"It's been an honor to know you," he tells me. "Tell your mother I'm sorry. Tell her -"

"She knows."

He smiles broadly and I watch as a warm, white light envelopes him.

"I will see you soon."

Chapter Sixteen
Earl

This is it. I inhale deeply, sucking in the rotten scent of the dead trees. Its slick floor is thick with mud as the rain falls hard at a forty-five degree angle. I had hoped to attack yesterday evening, as the sun set, blinding their watchtowers as we approached from the west, but a driving rain would suffice for cover now. Rain is all we've seen for the past three days and my army has become demoralized. It's now or never.

I'm not sure that I believe in destiny, but I know I was always meant to lead. Desperation breeds a need for stability, for leadership. In these uncertain times if you are not a leader of men you are nothing. I have little respect for those who would follow, and am comfortable labeling them expendable. It's good to be King! Lead with fear, and respect will follow. These people have lost everything: their families, their friends, and their self-respect. It is easy to lead a people so devastated. They are already fearful for their lives and the lives of those they love. They are starving and have no direction or purpose except to stay alive. So you bring that fear back, the fear of loss, of death. What do I have to offer? Purpose, for one. Protection in numbers and governance, something many of them remember from before the bombs. People want to be ruled. They want to be told they're doing a good job and that they are giving back to their community. They want to know there is a reason to go on, and that reason is the promise of something better, and that something is a base, packed with food, water, energy and shelter. When rallied, a group feeds off its leader, and off each other. And with the promise of salvation, they will follow you into Hell. But promises expire, and I see my army is restless. The time is now. What I've worked towards all these years is now upon me. My great purpose waits to be fulfilled.

Under a rudimentary tent of tarps tied securely to four tree trunks, I meet with my generals.

"Your teams are ready?" I ask them, my voice rising to be heard above the rat-a-tat-tat of rain slamming onto the taut tarp.

The four men nod in unison. Jonah, the oldest of my generals and approximately twenty years my senior, speaks up.

"I'm worried our plan won't work in this weather."

I glare at him. "This is not *our* plan, this is *my* plan, and if I say it will work, who are you to question that?"

Jonah steps back and straightens. "I meant no disrespect."

"Does your team share your concern?" I circle the four men.

"No." As he says this I can smell the fear on him. Good, I like that.

"This is no time to be making examples of my generals." I stop to face Jonah. "Do the rest of you feel my plan is flawed?"

"No, sir," they ring in. I keep my gaze on Jonah.

"You see, Jonah, you are wrong to be worried."

"I see that now." He avoids my stare.

"Good, good, then we will proceed as planned. Recall the scouts." With that, I order the men leave the security of the tent and rush back into the torrential weather, shouting orders. I had four scouts sent to the west wall, or more precisely, to the fox holes dug along the forest-line just twenty yards from the walls. They were dug under cover of night the past week and our scouts have been watching the towers for three days. We have been erecting siege weapons for the past month. I remembered the ancient siege tools that would launch dead enemies over the castle walls, as well as dead cattle and pigs to spread disease and fear among the residents. Though effective, we could not survive such an extended campaign, nor do I have the people to spare. Instead, I opted for siege towers and ladders to be built.

The scouts now back, they give us details concerning numbers at the towers, their shifts, and the best placement of our siege equipment. I discuss this with my generals and order the siege towers dragged just beyond the forest-line. The rain was falling so heavily now that it was becoming difficult to navigate the woods. But this was perfect, offering a visual distraction as well as muting the sounds we were making pushing over tree trunks as the equipment rolled clumsily through the sticky muck of the forest floor.

Upon passing the trenches we knew we were in place. Visibility was limited to about four or five yards, the west walls all but hidden behind sheets of rain. This bode well for the secrecy of our attack, but the scout's suggested points of entry were equally hidden.

My generals and I meet once more before the final charge. With four siege towers and a dozen ladders, we would be able to put one hundred soldiers inside the base before anyone was the wiser. The difficulty in this rain would prove itself once inside. Though each soldier has studied my rudimentary maps of the interior and been given a role in the attack, this rain prevented us from carrying out the plan to any degree of accuracy.

"Have each soldier stay put once they've landed inside. Unless we're made, we'll wait for the rain to let up." I say. "Let's make sure to take out any guards in their towers quietly," I make a quick gesture with my thumb running across my neck. "You pick the man in your teams to do the work. Let's do this shortly. Wait for the signal." With that we split up once more and I return to the siege tower which I will command personally.

The towers were made mostly of wood, a classic design I borrowed from medieval times. Four wheels sit under a heavily supported base and on that base walls are built along the front and two sides. Within the enclosure are two levels and ladders that go right to the top. At the top is a plank that will fall on hinges meeting the top of the wall and act as a bridge for my men to scale the wall and climb down on ropes.

The signal they wait on before beginning the siege would be a loud cracking sound, meant to mimic a falling tree, echoing through the woods.

My army was now at the walls and ready to pour in upon an unsuspecting community. I licked the rain water from my lips and thought of Sara and the things I would do to her before I let her die. A spastic smile works the muscles in my cheeks, the skin warming over from the action.

'SNAP'.

The signal sounds and echoes through the forest as planned. The siege towers move forward immediately and within a few seconds the equipment is in place. Silently we breach the walls and slide down on ropes. A thud indicates that a tower guard has been taken out.

Mid-siege the rain begins to taper off. The sheets of rain fall away like a curtain, revealing the base in all its detail. Moments later the sun shines down on the central parade grounds, a fog lifting, beckoning us on.

Chapter Seventeen
Earl

The sun burns up the fog, lifting it up and away, revealing the base in all its abundance. I am ready for action. I look to my right and see that my army is eager for the fight to begin. My generals are walking the line, their index fingers pressed up against their lips. On my signal we will move forward as one and fire at will.

Crack. Crack, crack, crack. My line scatters for cover as gun shots rain down on us. A siren sounds. The battle has now begun.

I duck behind a tree and take a moment to smell the bark and feel the rough surface. I smile, knowing that soon I will own this tree, and everything inside these walls. Then I detect a different scent, one familiar. Gasoline! As I make the connection, a flaming arrow lands a few yards from me in the soft forest floor, sparking a raging inferno. *Not again*. I scramble across the road and behind a large building, avoiding sporadic gun fire, and watch as others seeking refuge in the woods are flushed out by the fire and shot down.

"They're in the towers!" I scream to my platoon. We open up on the two eastern towers. Two bodies from each tower plummet to the saturated earth.

"Hold your fire!" I shout again. My orders are repeated four times down the length of the wall.

With the exception of the raging forest fire, the base goes silent once more. I listen for movement. I hear a metallic footfall, and reason that there are more soldiers on the roof of the building I am under. I whistle to my generals and point my finger to the sky. I then walk my fingers through the air to indicate that I hear men on the roof. They nod and prepare the pipe bombs. I throw one onto the roof of the hospital. Three more are lobbed up and I watch as the others toss theirs on the rooftops of the housing buildings and mess hall.

Explosions rain shrapnel onto my enemy. The sound of men screaming and shrapnel hitting the metal roofs excites me. Three soldiers fall from their high perch.

"Fire!" I scream. The three fallen soldiers have no time to react and are dead in seconds.

I send ten of my men to the roof to finish off anyone left, and report on our success. My generals follow my lead.

It's time to secure the grounds and move indoors.

More gun shots from above confirm that there were survivors and that they too are now dead. My group Captain leans past the roofs' overhang and I motion to him to send five men back and secure the grounds from his elevated position. As he obeys, more shots. I step aside in time to watch my Captain slam into the cement beside me with a sickening thud.

My men scatter again and fire into a Hummer which is now charging at us, a gunner on the big machine gun ripping my men apart. I steady my nerves and line the gunner up in my sights, snap off two rounds, and penetrate his helmet. I watch with satisfaction as he slumps over his gun and the Hummer slams on its breaks. Four doors open and gun barrels poke through the windows. I see a similar story playing out at the south end of the base as I slip behind a generator to avoid the hail of bullets. My men on the roof fire down on the unsuspecting soldiers, ending the exchange swiftly.

"Regroup!" I yell to my people still on the ground. As they huddle around me I realize I have lost a considerable number and am worried for the outcome. Either way, if I die today or take this base, today is the last day I want for anything, ever again.

"Let's move inside. I need you to remember your training. One kicks in the door and the other moves in. Then the kicker follows. Do this with each door you find, closets, anything." The men nod and kick in the back door to the hospital. I feel good about how the assault is progressing. Though worried I lost as many as I did right out of the gate.

Looking south I see my generals have begun the same process of flushing out anyone in hiding.

After twenty minutes the hospital is secure, but eerily quiet. I have confirmation from my generals that their buildings too are secure, and so I order men to the towers to lock down the perimeter. But where is everyone? The majority of the base's population - they must be hiding somewhere, the cowards. But they can't hide forever. We will find them. And take what we came for.

Chapter Eighteen
Leif

The majority of our people are safely situated on the eastern hill. The rain opens up rivers of mud on the hillside and impedes our view of the battle, soaking us through to our skins, but the sun now breaking through the clouds illuminates the central parade grounds, offering a clear picture of what is transpiring.

"Why did so many stay?" Mom steps out of one of the bunkers.

"The Sergeant told me, if he could save the base, he would try." He'd done what he had promised, rendering the generators useless, removing items Earl's army could never replace, and sending them up with our group. But his insistence in fighting the good fight, hoping to avert a full scale retreat, was either brave, or incredibly foolish if what I'd seen in my visions would come to pass.

In a short time the bomb would self-activate. If the Sergeant was left alive to stop it, he would send the flare. If not, the bomb would begin its countdown of one hour. I check my watch, which is synchronized with the bomb's timer.

My heart races at the possibility of the Sergeant actually turning the tides of destiny. He is a competent soldier and a good man, but the odds are stacked against him. Earl's forces are counted daily by the tower guards and the count holds at approximately two hundred. This number does not include the children, of which there are ten, none under the age of six. These children are currently being removed from Earl's camp by a separate task force, who will hide them in our lakeside gardens.

Blank Man has left me to my destiny. I see his light atop Castle Peak, waiting, watching.

The sound and smell of gun fire resonates over the wall of the base and climbs the hill, finding us, seventy refugees, watching the flashes of light pepper the landscape of our stronghold. Smoke begins to cloud our view of the battle as the woods and rooftops ignite and countless bullets leave hot barrels. I look at my watch. Five more minutes and the bomb will start its countdown. Five more minutes, Sergeant, to change our destiny.

"All is as it should be," I hear Blank Man whisper.

Daniel approaches mom and I. His expression is hopeful.

"How long?"

"Five minutes before the countdown starts." I am not without hope. But I am not without fear over my own end.

Mom hugs me, pressing her face against my back. "No flare yet."

"No flare," I repeat.

Chapter Nineteen
Earl

I am in the kitchen with my generals. We pull open the large fridges and freezers, our mouths watering. They are filled with food. I smile as I have not smiled in many, many years. My eyes squint as my cheeks burn at the unfamiliar act. I hide this reaction from my men, returning to my trademark scowl as I turn to meet them.

"Well, we've done it!" I pronounce, arms outstretched. The three men congratulate each other.

Suddenly the sound of gunfire in the kitchen sends us scrambling to the floor. Kent is shot in the chest, which spewing a cloud of blood in all directions. His body lands inches from Jonah, who's found shelter behind the metal island. The artillery fire ceases and I slip the pistol from my holster, slowly, quietly.

"Who's that?" I call out.

"The last voice you'll ever hear."

"We've got ourselves a live one here, boys!" I shout out. I need to flush this lone wolf out.

"Curtis?" I yell out.

"I'm here," he replies.

"Cover me!" I shout back.

Curt's head peers around the corner of the same island Jonah is hiding behind. He can see me too. I'm under the counter facing the line of industrial fridges, where I suspect our shooter is hiding.

Curtis looks questioningly at me. I point for him to stand and scan the area beyond me. Uunbeknownst to him, he will draw the shooter's fire.

I watch as he slowly rises to the level of the counter.

Pow! One shot and I hear Curt's head pop, and a split second later his corpse hits the tile floor behind me. I slip back behind the counter, having located our sniper's position.

My heart is racing now, but my nerves are steel. My excitement mounts as I deliberate on my next move.

"Jonah!" I call out. Nothing. No reply. This pisses me off. "Jonah, goddamn it, answer me!"

Three shots fire into the stainless steel counter inches from my head. I slide along the tile floor on my belly the length of the counter, spacing myself from the shooter.

"I'll fucking kill you myself when I'm done with this asshole if you don't answer me." I swear to Christ, I will too.

"I'm pinned down, Earl, what do you want me to do about it?"His voice is shaky.

"I want you to take out the shooter, Jonah. It's just one guy up there. He ain't goin' nowhere, either."

"I can't see him. Did you see what happened to Curt when you ordered him up?"

"Yeeeees, Jonah, I saw that. But you're not an idiot like Curt, now are you?"

A moment's pause. "No."

"So, what are you waiting for?"

I hear movement from behind the island. Jonah struggles to his feet, hoping to hit the shooter before he's shot himself.

"Where did you say he is?"

"I didn't say. He's above the fridges. Jammed back there like a sardine. All you have to do is let that automatic of yours do the work."

Once he starts firing I'll be able to pop up and zero in on the sniper, hopefully taking him out with a well placed shot.

Jonah starts counting. "Okay. One, two…"

"*Jesus*, don't count it out." I slam a fist into the steel cabinetry. "Are you dense or something?"

"Sorry."

"When you're ready just do it." I have no delusions that Jonah will live through this experience but Christ, he should at least give himself a fighting chance.

Then it happens. The automatic snaps off wild rounds, and I pounce. In my peripheral, I see Jonah's head snap back as the shooter finds pay-dirt. But this gives me the chance I need to line him up and fire two shots into the darkness above the cold storage.

I fall back below the counter tops and wait. Looking over to my right I see Jonah's head release a puddle of blood onto the white tile.

I wait another five minutes before picking myself up and inspecting my kill. I am leery of this, but without another general available to me, I do the work. I climb the metal ladder attached to one of the ice boxes to discover that my expert marksmanship has not let me down. It's a young man, shot in the face. I hit him with both shots! I slide the rifle from his death grip and hop down.

Once my feet hit the tile my knees buckle as I am struck in the face by a fist.

I stagger back and through blurry eyes see the face of an older man, dark hair layered with grey and a giant mole on his forehead. I shake my head trying to regain some semblance of equilibrium and narrowly escape another swing at my ringing head.

I pull my knife from its sheath on my leg and jab it at my attacker. Though I could skin a man alive, my fighting skills with a knife were amateurish at best.

My pistol, and the rifle I had just retrieved were lying on the floor, out of reach. Where did this guy come from?

I continue to swing my knife haphazardly and the man grabs my wrist, and twists it at an unnatural angle, snapping it. I suppress a scream. My free hand swings at his head but is expertly blocked. As my vision clears I realize who this man is.

"Sergeant," I say uncomfortably, one hand swaying uselessly at my side while the other remains in his grip.

"Earl," he hisses at me. The last time we saw one another was in the stockade, here on the base some ten years earlier.

"Did you know that guy?" I ask, realizing he was punishing me rather than just trying to kill me. But with this realization comes an opportunity. If I can talk to him, maybe one of my own people will charge in and shoot him down.

"My son," he says through clenched teeth. He follows through with another thundering punch to my temple and I go down. My head is buzzing so loudly now I don't know if I can keep up conversation.

"My family died defending this place," he continues. Then a boot comes down on my ribs. I groan at the pain. I remember a similar treatment ten years ago as his men worked me over for information.

"How did you know?" I manage to ask him, not sure that he'd know what I was talking about.

"Never mind how we knew, how you're going to die should be the only thing on your mind right now."

That was grim. Things are definitely looking grim for me right now. I'm not even sure I could stand to face him, and I truly believe my life depends on it.

"I don't care how I die, Sergeant." I swallow a mouthful of blood. "I only ever cared about how I lived."

The doors to the kitchen burst open and three of my men charge in, guns drawn.

"Get away from him!" one of them yells.

I hear myself laugh. My eyes close and I want to sleep. I lay down completely and watch the Sergeant's face screw up into a hate I know too well.

He pulls his weapon and fires on my men. In turn he is shot a dozen times. Some hit his body armor, but others find his shoulders, arms, legs and finally, his neck. He falls gracefully to his knees and as his head tilts forward, his chin tucks into his chest and blood rushes out of his mouth.

"Are you alright?" The remaining soldier bends over me.

"Help me up." I lift a hand and he takes it. I am beyond dizzy, but can manage. I realize there may be others embedded in the tight spaces and dark corners waiting to ambush my men.

As we move outside a hush comes over those gathered. They see me bruised and battered, my wrist unnaturally bent to the right.

"You should see the other guy," I say in an attempt to lighten the mood. They laugh, still giddy in light of our victory.

"We have rats in the walls," I announce. "They may all still be here, waiting to ambush us, to divide and conquer. This war ain't over yet. I want groups of six to run through every inch of this base. Be smart, be silent and flush them out."

*****

As I watch the groups, twelve in all, set off to flush out what infestation may remain, the realization of what I have accomplished excites me. The throbbing in my wrist subsides. From such humble beginnings I now hold the ultimate position of power. I have overthrown my enemy; taken control of the most sought after piece of real-estate within a thousand miles and am the leader of a great army. Pride cannot describe what I am feeling. I no longer have to ask myself whether it was dumb luck that landed me on that camping trip so many years ago, surviving the initial end my family suffered. There is no question now that destiny has led me here, that my actions and the actions of those who subsisted with me blazed this path. After the vote had been cast to make Joel our leader, after the fire Sara set at the house, after months living at the barn garden and the numerous attempts to disrupt this base's infrastructure, I am victorious. After my confinement here and my escape, after another ten long years of scraping by and building my army the end I knew I was fated to realize, has been.

*****

Another twenty minutes passes and I count only three gunshots. Perhaps they have fled.

Chapter Twenty
Earl

Where is *Sara?* They must have rushed everyone out to the lake. Are they hiding in their gardens? How did they know I would attack today? These questions plague me, taking away from this great victory I should be enjoying. I want to *kill* Sara. I've wanted that as much as I have wanted to take this base. Well, one out of two ain't so bad, considering. But that snot-nosed kid of hers, Leif, I wanted to take him out of the game too. Preachy little prick. Okay, one out of three is nothing to be proud of. We would finish securing the base and I would send a platoon to the lake to be sure.

My face and wrist have been dressed with what was left in the hospital storage lockers. A splint would have to do for now, where my broken wrist is concerned.

The Captain from Kirk's group runs up to me. "Earl, the equipment is missing components."

"Missing…"

He rushes me to the open generator, and I realize what he means by *missing*. A particular component that is crucial in the operation of these units is gone. And it is very clear that it is not something we could just replace. All of the generators were missing the same piece and so all of the windmills and solar panels and even the gas powered motors were utterly useless.

"Goddamn it." I'm so pissed off. This is half a victory. They've robbed me of power. "How in the fuck did they know we were coming?"

The four men were dumbstruck. I knew none of them could produce an answer.

Chapter Twenty-one
Leif

I spot Dieter as he emerges from the bunker.

"Dieter," I greet him, tapping nervously at my watch.

"Leif," he replies with a tired smile. He takes me by the arm, guiding me toward a large flat stone and seating us there.

"I had - how do you say - an epiphany!" Dieter tells me excitedly. "Just last night."

"Like an idea?"

"Yes, but more than that, it's like an idea has just been confirmed as fact, rather than just a theory." Dieter's aura is pulsating a golden hue of inner knowledge.

"Tell me, can it help us now?" I wave Daniel over.

"It will help you further understand the connection science and spirituality share. It might not help us out of our immediate danger, but if we should survive... Even if we don't..." I prepare myself for another revealing lecture from this brilliant man. Daniel kneels in front of us and listens.

"You experience visions, yes?" I nod affirmatively. "What is a vision?" he asks.

"A future event. Something that could occur based on all that has led to that moment." I think back on all the angel has shown me.

"Exactly. And what are you doing in order to see this information?" He shifts excitedly on the stone slab.

"It's shown to me in meditation, by my guide in the spiritual world."

"Right, exactly. And what have I told you about the spiritual world?"

"That it is the same as the quantum world, the very small."

"Right. So, let me explain my epiphany. Before the bombs fell, we, the scientific community, were just beginning to experiment with the idea of time travel. Actually passing information through time via neutrinos."

"Neutrinos?" Another new word.

"Yes, they are an invisible particle that lives in the quantum world. In fact, we are being bombarded by millions of them right now, passing through us at the quantum level." He waves his hands wildly. "But, I digress! You see, the experiment had been tested many times, and the results were always the same. Every time a group of neutrinos were fired from a source to a specific destination, it was confirmed that they had travelled faster than the speed of light! And if something can go faster than the speed of light, it becomes a future event. Suddenly Einstein's theory that nothing in the universe can travel faster than light is questioned. All of physics is suddenly being put under the microscope, so to speak."

I am stunned by this incredible description of what mankind was on the brink of discovering about the natural world, and that we had been so close to understanding so much. Dieter notices my state of awe and slaps me twice on the arm.

"Do you see how this further develops my theory on the spiritual plane and the quantum plane existing as one idea, one unified theory? Think about it, Leif, nothing should be able to travel faster than the speed of light. So where are the neutrinos going? Another dimension? A wormhole? They must be taking an alternate route to the destination than the rest of us. Nothing travels faster than light. This is what we know. But the neutrino says differently. And you, my friend, say differently. When you leave space-time during meditation to travel into the future to experience your visions, events not yet realized in the material world, your consciousness is traveling faster than light - reporting on a future event!"

I close my eyes and shake my head. This is truly inspiring.

"Isn't it amazing? Even after science had lost the ability to experiment with new theories, years later, I come upon you. Living proof."

"Everything is for a reason." I say, a sense of purpose taking hold. I fill up with the overwhelming urge to live, to keep going.

I watch a tear track the deep lines in Dieter's face. He looks past me and then up to the sky, where a perfect blue is framed by the rising smoke escaping the base.

"I have proven my theories work, without so much as a laboratory." A rising lump in his throat can be heard in his speech. "I have found the theory of everything."

Breaking the moment, Mom takes me by the arm and leads me away. We walk a few yards and stop. The sounds of gun shots still pierce the air intermittently. Shouts from Earl's army are vulgar and filled with hateful elation.

She turns me to face her, grasping my arms in her hands as I watch tears well up in her eyes.

"We've lost the base, Leif. We've lost everything."

"Not everything," I grab her arms and squeeze. "We still have our lives. And we have each other."

"I *love you*, Leif," she says. She's said it a thousand times before, but this time is different. This time she says it with a sense of finality that makes me heartsick.

"I love you, Mom." I nervously look at my watch, realizing the bomb should have blown the base sky high. But it hadn't. The digital output is frozen at nine seconds. I move to leave, but mom grabs my arm.

"Leif, don't." She pleads.

I turn and face her, she is crying now. I didn't want this moment with her. I didn't want to say goodbye.

"Whatever it is," she pauses. "Whatever it is you're going to do, don't. Please." She takes my face in her hands. What is it she thinks she knows?

"Mom," I manage. "Mom, please." Now I'm the one doing the pleading. "I have to go." I shake my head and she pulls me close and hugs me. I hug her back.

"I love you." She says again, pulls away and takes my hands in hers. "You're my baby." She tells me through heavy sobs. "Let me do what needs to be done."

"It's not yours to do, Mom." I insist, trying to keep from crying. "It's alright, Mom." My voice lowers to a whisper. "All is as it should be."

"Leif, please. You're just a boy."

My heart hardens at this final appeal. I've never been just a boy. I've never felt like other boys my age, ever. I'd been born into servitude. Reared to complete a destiny I couldn't carry out in a past life. To hear my Mother say 'I'm just a boy' is heartbreaking, but also exactly what I needed to hear.

"Mom, you know I'm not. You've always known." I squeeze her hands and let go. "I love you. And I will see you soon." I smile at her, turn and walk away.

Chapter Twenty-two
Leif

The bomb has not ignited. Daniel's face is set in stone. Swallowing hard, he looks back at the base. "This is it then," he says, looking at my digital watch.

"Yes," I nod. The realization that I had been bred for this end was bittersweet. Especially in light of what Dieter had just discovered. I so desperately want to continue my spiritual journey here, on this plane. Teach the science behind the spiritual and appeal to everyone's sense of purpose.

"It's just as we'd seen."

I concentrate on my aura and let it envelope us both, giving him strength.

"Stay with our friends and family now, Daniel. They *need* you."

"They need *you*, Leif! Not me! Who am I?"

"Who am *I*, Daniel?" I grasp the back of his head and pull him closer. "*Who am I?* I'm just like you," I whisper. "I'm *afraid*, Daniel." I release him once more and back off.

I take up the binoculars and study my route to return to the base. My plan B. Earl's forces are crawling all over the base now, but I have a secret infiltration point, one the Sergeant and I had mapped out when the bomb had been constructed. Should I make it down the hill undetected, I would make it to the bomb.

I pan the temporary bunkers, where supplies have been dumped in preparation for this possible end. I see fear on the faces of the crowd gathering at the hill's crest.

Turning back to Daniel I tell him what he already knows. "Keep them here. Keep them safe. Teach them what you know."

Daniel nods. I lay a hand on his shoulder, then cup the back of his neck and squeeze. "You're ready."

Chapter Twenty-three
Leif

On my descent towards the base my face flushes with fear. Thoughts of fleeing, of turning back, of returning to my life, plague me. The closer I get to the base, the stronger the impulse is.

The Blank Man can be heard in my head once more as I question this path one final time.

"Death brings an honest response," he says.

Had I heard this before? I continue down the slope on all fours to escape detection, sliding in the mud on my hands and knees. "What are you saying?" I whisper. What response should I have in death?

"Remember what death is."

Death is a release from this life, from pain, sadness, angst and hate.

"What else?" This is a strange time for a conversation, but I'll bite.

It is an opportunity to live again, either in this life, or in the next. To know death is a gift. To know what it is, and to understand it allows you to approach death as you would a friend.

"How will you greet death?"

I will meet death with arms open, heart full and the knowledge that this life is fleeting, impermanent, but necessary and important. My response to death is to embrace it, to respect it and to understand it. As life is full of purpose, so is death. Memories are of the ethereal, and not the material world, that is how I know I am forever.

Soon I am back at the east wall, the sounds of gunshots still exploding over the victorious shouts from within. I open a trap door that takes me beneath the watch tower and follow the underground crawl space for ten minutes, fighting off bouts of claustrophobia, until I enter the dry storage directly under the kitchen. I push through the ventilation hatch and climb on to the smooth concrete floor.

The bomb sits a few feet from me. Its size is comically massive. As I approach the monstrosity I see that sure enough, the yellow wire has popped off its position behind the timer, stopping the process at just nine seconds. I wonder, perhaps for the final time if this is my only option. So much death. Could we not perhaps live? Continue running, fleeing Earl's army, hoping for and expecting much better for the future. No children had been born in years. I know the human population is already on the brink of expiring. But still, was it not our inherent nature to hope? Were we not given this ability for a reason? Even if 'death' could bring peace, should we not still choose life?

A realization overcomes me: I am standing in my final resting place, my mausoleum. My life would end precisely nine seconds after I replace the wire.

I take several deep, cleansing breaths, then climb up onto the steel table and sit directly behind the bomb.

"*Son of a bitch!*" The voice is Earl's. I look up, past the bomb. He is poking his head into the stairwell, which descends from the kitchen floor.

My destiny so clear now, I can taste purpose in the very air around me. I know there is nowhere he can run.

Our eyes lock as he watches me place the wire to the back of the timer, and the clock move backwards from 9, 8, 7…

Epilogue

In that short time afforded me, I relive my final conversation with my angel. The moment so still, and poignant, as the timer continues its countdown: 6, 5, 4… I am standing once more on Castle Peak, Blank Man having just revealed my destiny.

"So, this is to be my end? Like my father's end."

"This end was never in question, Leif. Your father carried it out prematurely and without purpose."

"I'm having some trouble with this end, friend."

"But you understand it is the end you were meant to arrive at."

"I do."

"Then rejoice, and know that everything you have accomplished brought you to this end."

"I understand. But I am afraid."

"Why? After all you know, all you've been shown?"

"Human nature I guess." I smile up at him.

"Leave this behind you."

"Enlighten me again, friend. What was it all for?"

"Our identities have been hidden in the flesh and blood and ambition of humanity long enough. Those who have come back again and again and not learned their greater purpose will be discarded in this final exodus from the flesh."

"To have lived so many lives, how could every soul not know love?" I ask, dumbfounded.

"It is a question those souls will be asking themselves for an eternity."

"We cannot save them?" I plead.

"They have made their choice," he replies, his voice soft and sad.

"We're finished then."

"You've only just begun."

Additional Resources:

www.the-judas-syndrome.com- official website for the series

More books by Michael Poeltl

The Judas Syndrome (Book one)
Rebirth (Book two of The Judas Syndrome)
Her Past's Present
Available on Amazon

About the author

Website: www.mikepoeltl.com
Twitter: @mpoeltlauthor
Facebook: Michael.Poeltl.author
Amazon Author Page: Michael Poeltl Amazon

Acknowledgements

Rose Keefe – Editor - www.rosekeefe.com
Thanks once more to my editor and friend, Rose, as she continues to assist me in my journey.

www.ingramcontent.com/pod-product-compliance
Lightning Source LLC
Chambersburg PA
CBHW020129180626
46810CB00004B/1462